VIA Folios 79

ONLY SONS

ONLY SONS

FRED MISURELLA

BORDIGHERA PRESS

Library of Congress Control Number: 2012935823

The characters and events in this novel are fictitious. Any similarity to real persons, living or dead, is coincidental and not intended by the author.

Printed in the United States.

Published by
BORDIGHERA PRESS
John D. Calandra Italian American Institute
25 W. 43rd Street, 17th Floor
New York, NY 10036

VIA Folios 79
ISBN 978–1–59954–042–9

For Kim and Alex,
                              with love.

And for two who have shown the way:

Daniela Gioseffi and Anthony Tamburri,
                           amici.

We trembled at the sight that met us,

of everything changed and piled high

with ashes like snow.

— Pliny the Younger

CONTENTS

SONNY

1.

"Dad, do you like it?" Franco asked. "Is everything all right?"

"Sure," Sonny said, looking at his son. "I just wish your grandmother could be here. And. . . ."

"Mom?"

"Of course."

You turn a page, look in the mirror, try to remember a face. Suddenly more than twenty years have passed. Sonny Salvaggi's son, Franco, had not yet become the doctor he was meant to be, but, having graduated college, he was no longer a boy. Franco extended his arm, sweeping in the house of his fiancée, Roseanna Sabastianni, their family garden, juniper trees, rose bushes, and hedges, the high brick wall, all sealing off his wedding from the rest of Smithfield. In the distance beyond the house, Maresciallo's Mountain loomed above them like a ghostly pile of cinder, limestone, and shale. At the time people might have envied it, but they have changed their minds a little since.

"Why shouldn't I like it?" Sonny said. "Everything. . . . It's perfect."

Inhaling his cheroot, he slapped his son on the back, hearing a hum of strings rise in the background while a double bass thumped at some popular song that the guests, in particular Roseanna's baby sisters, danced to. Years would pass, decades even, but Sonny would recall how profoundly that music affected him, especially the chilling, whiny voice of the bandleader calling out above his fellow musicians:

"Come on, bai-ee-bee, less do the twissst!"

Not Italian obviously, not from Sicily or Basilicata, not even from the Tuscan north. He knew little of this music, nothing except that it did not belong to him, his people, or his era. "No *tarantella* at this wedding," Franco had muttered. "Roseanna's parents won't have us stamping out the devil."

"*Medigahns,*" Sonny thought. But for some reason the music that night exerted magic, enticing Sonny to dance for the first time since Lina had died. And he wasn't alone. As the music blared, piano and drum thumping as if prompted by a metronome, a young girl in a yellow dress appeared. She smiled from the crowd, approached, her lips pink, and crooked a finger at him, nodding. Without a word, she moved her feet with Sonny's. Then she took his hands, held both out to the side, and, as if they were flying, pulled Sonny along with her, swiveling her hips and nodding to Franco, until they got to the middle of the patio.

"You certainly move smoothly enough for this," she said, leaning forward and drawing him closer among the other couples. "You follow the music easily."

"For an old geezer," Sonny replied, "and a wop one, at that."

He blushed as she shook out her hair, extended her arms so that her palms touched his hips, and pressed them each alternately — left, right, left, right — in rhythm with the music. As if she were an ocean wave carrying him toward the shore, Sonny felt his body yielding to her movement.

"Good," the young woman said. "This is working."

Slim, red-haired, wearing a slightly disheveled, still lovely yellow gown ("Sallie Ann's," she would tell him later). Dressed in immaculate pumps and tails, Sonny weighed, as usual at the time, a solid one hundred and eighty pounds. Yet, like his heart in that cool summer air, his body floated lightly above his feet.

"Why don't you dance with somebody your own age?" he blurted, embarrassed for the moment. "With Jack, or even Franco?"

"What's wrong with mature men?" she said, quietly. "I like them older, too."

"Graying and slightly balding, I imagine."

She shook her head, her pink face blanching, then with a secret smile spun around and away from Sonny. She raised her hands, clapped them in a sudden burst of energy, shook her hips, and sang to the music.

"Margo," he said, drawn closer to her now. "That's your name — isn't it?"

She nodded and for a moment stepped within his arms, her breasts brushing against his chest.

"A very pretty name. Lovely, in fact."

"Old — like all the important men in my life."

Margo smiled. He saw her hair flash when she tossed her head. Perfect in the lights, the color framed her face and soft pale lips with a quiet, burnished flame. Within his gradually lightening mood (he had drunk a small amount of wine), Sonny felt his heart turn into smoke.

"You have a good memory," Margo whispered, touching him. "I'm impressed."

"Hey, I'm not senile. Besides, I always make a point to remember Jack's girlfriends. Especially their names."

"Just their names?"

He waved, grinning at her look, and spun around himself, although he was careful not to let the weight shift too abruptly at his ankles.

"They are always beautiful," Sonny said. "And though I'm moving on and up, I'm certainly not a fool — at least when it comes to women."

Margo's eyes widened; in the pale light her skin seemed to glow even more. At first Sonny thought she was angry, because when he embraced her at that moment she stiffened and pushed him away. But just as quickly she relaxed, murmuring, "Oh, I admire people like you," and let out a long, luxurious sigh. Sonny stepped closer, feeling Margo's hair then her face brush against his chest. Then breasts again. . . . At first he thought she was teasing, but he thought of the way she had looked earlier, that morning in fact, and felt pleased. And then, of course, he inhaled her perfume.

2.

She had arrived with Jack Maresciallo in a 1950 Studebaker, motoring over the Alleghenies into the Poconos and, finally, worn and sleepy, rumbling through the gates of the Sabastianni compound at about ten a.m.

"From Ohio," Franco had said, smiling.

Jack emerged from the car stretching his arms and, after shaking out his dark, curly locks, embraced Franco like a brother, with much happy laughter and slapping of backs. He kissed Sonny's cheek and, returning to the car, pulled Margo from the passenger's side. With the soft, penetrating scent of patchouli emerging from the car ahead of her, Jack offered her up to his hometown world as if she were a special gift he had brought for them.

"Sonny, this is Margo. Margo, Sonny Salvaggi. He's the only person I know who's as smart as — no, smarter than — Franco."

Sonny nodded and immediately eyed the young woman from head to toe. The strong fragrance stormed his nostrils — a touch of spring, the warmer breeze of summer — yet he knew the other women at the wedding — Italians — would likely shake their heads and say it smelled too strong. "Pushy," they'd say. "What's she got to sell?"

Wide-eyed, Margo struck Sonny as frail at first. Fond as he was of Jack, admiring the many lovely young women he had introduced to Franco in high school and college, including his daughter-in-law, Rose-anna, Sonny Salvaggi thought at first that Jack could do better, *should* do better, in fact.

Narrow-shouldered, Margo possessed a pleasing smile and nicely turned-up breasts that seemed to increase her stature. And she acted ac-cordingly, at least in Franco's opinion. At the Ohio college they all had attended, Franco said, Margo gave Jack more than he could handle, with other men as well as with her studies. Her face showed something com-bative in that morning light: serious, aloof, not consistent with his expec-tations, even when her eyes, alert for a moment, looked deeply into his, as if for personal contact. Young, Sonny thought, but not naïve. Margo attracted men, was not entirely happy in knowing it, and, because of that, floated, like her perfume, on very agitated air. In fact, Sonny thought to himself later that night, she reminded him of Jack's mother, Lillian. A man might be tempted, but the challenge would not be ordinary.

"Franco's smarter than his old man," Sonny said to Jack. "Or soon will be — though perhaps not with the ladies."

He bowed, grinning, took Margo's hand, and removing the cheroot, placed his lips against the back of her fingers. Margo curtsied, murmuring thanks, but smiled crookedly when Sonny straightened and looked at her face. In jeans and a wrinkled denim shirt with an embroidered red and green rose on the breast pocket, she managed to affect the gracious aloof-ness of a poor gentlewoman, even if a bit edgy and tired from the trip.

"You old lecher! Stop slobbering!" Jack said to him, guffawing.

He punched Sonny's shoulder, and, grabbing for his right forearm and falling forward, began to giggle. It had been a game since Jack's boyhood to take Sonny's hand and arm, lean on them and, by surprise, try to pull Sonny off his feet. Failing (he always did), Jack would take the hand in both of his own and try, with feigned moaning and grunting, to crush it. Tall and muscular when he was twelve, Jack could palm a basketball but never quite gathered the leverage or strength to unbalance Sonny or make him wince. Twenty-one now, he tried again but still failed, and so, smiling as was *his* custom after Jack's initial efforts, Sonny suddenly lurched to his left as Jack leaned against him and effortlessly, painlessly jerked him to the ground. Then he squeezed Jack's fingers, hard.

"Enough! Enough! Sonny, yiii! — That hurts!"

On his side in the grass, Jack moaned, genuinely, even as he laughed in pain.

"You are still not big enough. Or strong enough. And my fingers are not made of paper."

From the ground Jack glanced at Margo, then Sonny, and laughed again. A broad smile creased her face as Jack leaped effortlessly to his feet, but it meant nothing that Sonny could understand. She turned to Franco who, without a word, stepped closer, frowning.

"Dad, Roseanna and her parents are coming out any minute. Father Dan will be with them. Let's try to put on a respectable performance."

Sonny blushed, dusting a speck from his trouser leg. Margo stepped closer to Jack, barely acknowledging their silliness, and helped him straighten his hair. Sonny doffed his hat and bit on the cheroot.

"My son for you," he muttered to Margo. "The old man embarrasses him. Always has. I hope I haven't embarrassed you."

She said nothing, barely nodded, certainly not looking directly at him.

"Are you that way with *your* father, young lady? The truth!"

Margo laughed, dryly. But her eyes turned dark as Jack tightened his belt, straightened his hips, and turned to Franco. At that moment Roseanna opened the door to her house and gave out a happy cry. "Jack! Margo! — And everybody! How are you?"

Delighted with the world — and her life, apparently — Roseanna nearly danced into the yard when she saw them, beaming at the sun, the flowers, the imminent summer in the bracing morning air. Her cheeks glowed. Sonny saw the Sabastianni parents emerge from the house behind her, and then he spotted their priest, a slight, tall, dark-haired young man, new to the parish and known, to some people's disappointment, as a clerical liberal. Sonny had seen the priest bowling down at the Garibaldi Club with several of the women one night. Giggling and laughing like a schoolboy, he had worn no collar, just the black trousers and shoes with a simple white shirt. Sonny had watched the priest drink beer and blush while rolling balls into the gutter; then he heard the loud screams and giggles of the women. Once or twice, Sonny

observed, Father Dan had placed a friendly arm around one of the
women's shoulders, and later he left for home in the company of three
of them. Safe, the Garibaldi men had gossiped jealously, safer than some
older, married — or widowed — man. Yes, he probably prefers the boys.

"Dad," said Roseanna, flashing a smile as she embraced Sonny
warmly and kissed his cheek, "you know Father Dan Moro, don't you?"

"I have seen him." Sonny nodded as the two shook hands. "Nice to
meet you formally, Father."

"Ah, *Signore Salvaggi*. We owe our new gymnasium floor to you, I
believe. A major donation. Please call me Dan."

Sonny bowed, and Franco introduced Margo and Jack to everyone.
After several minutes, Father Dan walked everyone through the wedding ceremony. It would take place that evening on the Sabastianni
grounds within a beautiful bower surrounded by lilacs and wisteria. On
either side of the trellises two horse chestnut trees rose toward the sky
while a line of poplars and hedge stood in back of them. Two servants
set up white folding chairs in the open space before them, and while
Franco, Jack, and Sonny stood beneath the wisteria, others brought out
long tables and linen for the dinner. They would be set up near the
flower garden under the poplars.

The ceremony was unusual in that both Sonny and Jack — as double
best men — would stand beside Franco and present the rings as the couple took their vows. During the rehearsal Margo squatted against a tree
and smoked while Roseanna's father, Tomaso, red-faced and smiling,
escorted his daughter toward the groom. From behind her, an organ
hummed softly, mixing with the quiet buzz of the bees in the wisteria,
as members of the wedding party waited and smiled.

3.

"Heavenly Father, we are gathered here . . ."

Father Moro said that several times. In the morning, he stopped
abruptly, smiled, and silently led the party through the rest of the rehearsal
step by step. Later, during the real ceremony, as his words rumbled
through the warm night air, Sonny Salvaggi glanced at Jack by his side

and then over his shoulder at some two hundred seated guests and twenty or more servants standing behind them. Within the crowd, he spotted Jack's father, Anthony Maresciallo, alone in the fifth row with a dark suit and a red rose in his lapel. "Like a don," Sonny whispered. "An enemy."

Yet he felt proud — of his son, the two families, their evident taste in the lovely outdoor ceremony, the warm personality of Franco's bride, and especially the love Franco had demonstrated by bringing his father to the altar with his bride. Margo sat in the same row as Anthony, but at the far end away from him. In her yellow gown, with her red hair and freckled shoulders attractively bare, she seemed perfectly in place, while Anthony, neighbor and former family friend, looked absolutely out of place and uncomfortable. Sonny enjoyed Anthony's isolation, knowing the man's eye (and need) for social company — especially of women — was at least as urgent as his own. When he danced with Margo to that crazy, whining, young people's music shortly afterward, Sonny tried his best to rub it in.

"How do you find it?" he asked, grasping Margo's soft arms while she swiveled before him. "Does it please you?"

"Of course. I love to dance."

"And the wedding — this party?"

She nodded dreamily, spinning and leaving Sonny's hands so he couldn't pull her closer.

An instant later, she returned, shaking her shoulders and her breasts. "I'm impressed with everything I've seen today. Especially here."

"Here?"

Margo smiled.

"And you've seen Maresciallo's, haven't you? The house, the mountain."

She smiled, nodding. "The big house, and bigger mountain." She paused, waving her hand. "Now that was *really* impressive, I must admit. And named after them!"

Sonny grinned. "So you've formally met the *padrone*, Anthony, as well, and seen his holdings."

"Holdings? —"

"Yes. Anthony's. Buildings and land. I built most of them, you know."

Margo laughed. With a little sigh, she bumped Sonny's hips on her own, caught his damp hands for an instant, and twirled away again, just as he sought to embrace her. "Certainly — and we stopped in for a glass of delicious wine this afternoon. Homemade!"

Looking over her head, Sonny clutched her wrist and, as Margo moved nearer, gathered her comfortably into his arms. To his surprise, she relaxed in his warmth, leaning against his chest. He felt old, but for-tunate-holding a bud to his bosom: perhaps not quite ready to bloom.

But almost.

"You must come to my house," Sonny said. "It's not far — up the road from Maresciallo's. You must come for dinner before you leave."

Margo grinned, more in awkwardness than genuine interest, it seemed.

"Please," Sonny said. "I think you'd enjoy it."

She looked away as if — as if, Sonny hated to admit, she didn't want to believe him. He sighed.

"Why?" she asked, then spun away again.

"Why not?" He moved forward, trying to touch her bare arms. "Are you afraid?"

Shrugging, Margo nodded, her pale face a mask, a neutral one. "Jack will be there. What would we do?"

"What would we do?" He blurted. "I can cook. I can tell you some good Anthony Maresciallo stories. And I have very good wine."

Margo grinned at that, though clearly still not really intrigued. Soon the music slowed. As she looked toward Jack's table, Sonny found her arms again. He pressed against her, his hand on her warm shoulder blades, his chest just touching her breasts. He attempted a clumsy, old-fashioned waltz, even as the music surged. The blood rushed to his face as the moonlight, now turning purple in the dark, illuminated a trans-parent haze behind her. The breeze quickened. In one corner near the poplars, Anthony Maresciallo sat at a table alone, frowning. Sonny saw him lean back and fold his hands across his belly. Franco, a husband now, sat at the head table with Father Moro and Roseanna, while the Sabastiannis talked to relatives behind them. With his usual enthusiasm, Jack paid attention to everything in the world around him, but nothing of importance to himself.

"Come alone," Sonny whispered, inhaling lavender in the evening breeze. "Tomorrow — after sunset. I would like you to."

"You can't be serious! What will I do with Jack?"

She laughed abruptly, a deep, throaty sound, surprisingly mature.

"Of course I'm serious. Send him on an errand." Sonny stumbled as they turned. "What have I been talking about?"

Margo shook her head. "I have no idea. Really."

"Is it absurd for an old man to be interested in a beautiful woman? To want to see her? To dine . . ."

She laughed again, brazenly, calling attention to herself — and, of course, him. The blood rushed more quickly to his face, and Sonny could not look at Anthony then —"Pig, fatter than me — fatter than anyone here!" he thought — sitting beneath the trees, studying an old friend.

"But I thought we might be staying with you tonight anyhow," Margo said. "Jack thought —"

"With *me* — Jack?"

"I don't think he's arranged anything with his father. He — They — They don't —"

"Get along!" Sonny held up his hand. "Say no more! I'll be delighted."

She cringed.

"We'll have more than dinner together," Sonny said. "You'll see the way an Italian gentleman lives — in America."

She laughed, roaring now, her mouth open in a thunderous, throaty "O."

"Gentleman — I'll bet!"

She hummed the music louder, an unreadable expression flitting across her face. Yet her eyes flashed, Sonny saw, with unspeakable flirtations.

Margo put her arms on his shoulders, linking her fingers behind his neck. Then, as the music accelerated into another twisting tune, she stepped back, took Sonny's hands, planted her feet, and started to swivel her hips. Her hair floated across her eyes, shimmering; flecks of purple from the risen full moon made it glow.

Sonny followed her when she moved, swiveling his own hips as best he could while Margo backed across the dance floor. He watched Anthony Maresciallo drum his stiff fingers against his stomach and, enjoying the moment, threw his head back, spread his arms, and crooned with the awful, awful singer, "Ooooh, ooooh! Bai-beee! Let's . . ."

The scent of lilac, wisteria, and another, sweeter perfume filled Sonny's head with the dreamy memory of women and, as in a younger time, the greater sweetness of dealing with others as they had once stooped to deal with him.

LILLIAN

4.

Anthony knew that Sonny had been with her, of course. After the horse calmed and the driver reined it over to the curb, Sonny was the first at her side, and he gave the police an eyewitness account of the accident, the horse, the wagon, the boy darting into the street, the mother darting after him. As he talked, he held little Jack, screaming against his chest, covering the boy's eyes so he wouldn't see his mother's bloody body or the marks of the wheels in the street. The ambulance took her, still alive but unconscious, to the hospital across town. She died there the following afternoon, with Sonny and Anthony in attendance, glaring at each other in the waiting room when the doctor walked in to break the awful news.

Out of consideration for a dead friend and her son, all the members of the Garibaldi Club attended her funeral. Difficult as Lillian had been, she had loved (and been loved by) everyone. They all felt they owed her something, even though her Irish-Tuscan family was not strictly one of their own. She had made countless gifts of fruit, flowers, crafts, and vegetables. She had knitted beautiful sweaters, scarves, and mittens. She had driven all the children wearing those items to the church school from time to time, fed them lunches when neither mother nor father could, and taken them for Saturday afternoon trips into the mountains where they hunted mushrooms, wildflowers, and herbs, and occasionally sketched. Certainly, Sonny knew, Lillian had showed more love to his son, Franco, than Anthony showed Jack after the accident — and more to him, some hinted, than she showed her own husband and maybe even Jack in life.

"A lovely, imperfect human being," Sonny always said of her. "Like the rest of us. But deep."

"I'll hang on — for Jack," Lillian had whispered to Sonny just before she died.

Of course they had been lovers, briefly, but before that he had often talked to her as a cousin — even a sister — because she was very important to him. She had taught him to read poetry, listen to music, enjoy art. And so, when Sonny found her alone in her studio one afternoon, sobbing while Franco and Jack played in the nearby kitchen pantry, he sat next to her and asked, with deep earnestness, if he or any of their friends could help. Lillian shook her head, moaning. He urged her to talk, and when he moved closer, his arm circling her shoulders, Lillian inclined her head to his chest, sobbed, and let her anger and frustration pour out in a stream of tears. She revealed what Sonny, and many others, already knew: She mentioned Boris Corcoran, the art teacher she still loved, of course, and the complications of his other women. Sonny had realized that bringing Franco to visit Jack so often probably added to her burdens, but a few months before, Lillian had practically begged him to continue. Franco was a help, she insisted, not a burden. He took her mind off more pressing romantic problems. Besides, Franco calmed Jack, she said, allying with her whenever Jack, spirited and athletic, lost control. Sonny admired that in his son, even as he searched for signs that Franco might turn a little wild himself. On the contrary, Franco grew more polite, showing genuine civility and kindness well beyond his years at home and elsewhere. That touch again, the one that had changed him, from Lillian.

"Lillian's influence," Sonny said about Franco. "Her gentle style and unselfishness have moved across a bloodline."

Yet despite her mild, generous nature, despite her beauty, she had to suffer the shame of Anthony's coldness and the teacher Corcoran's other adventures.

"Are you sure I can't help?" he asked. "It wouldn't work if I spoke to Anthony. He doesn't trust me. But maybe if I spoke to . . . Carmine —"

She shook her head sharply at the mention of that name — her father-in-law's. "Carmine approves of it," she said. "Everything. He sees the insult against him and his family honor."

"But Jack, the boy—"

She raised her hands. "They have never forgiven me for Boris Corcoran, Sonny. After all this time."

"Or the name," Sonny said. "Jack's. They'll always think —"

She shook her head again, angrily. There had been a lot of talk, of course. At the Garibaldi Club, Lillian's behavior around Corcoran seemed obvious. Yet some people, especially the women, forgave her that; Anthony, condescending and cold, deserved the horns, they said. But who would tell Lillian that on the principle of names almost no one, especially at the Garibaldi Club, would take her side? In the poorer villages of southern Italy, the *Mezzogiorno*, where most of the club members had lived or counted ancestors, a name, first and last, is often the only possession a family can pass on. The boy's name should have been Carmine's or, at least, Anthony's.

"They will get over it," Sonny told her, though he assumed no one really would — not in their lifetime.

"John Boris Maresciallo. What's done is done," Lillian said. "Even Carmine has to see that."

Sonny frowned. At that moment Jack and Franco burst into the room, both howling that the other boy had held onto a toy — a truck, a game, or some important trinket — for too long. Lillian grinned, prying the toy from their grips before tossing it gently to Franco. "He's visiting, Jackie; let him have it. Learn to be generous."

Jack howled, louder, and she kneeled, embracing him.

"Honey, he's your best friend. He always has been. Treat him like a brother." Lillian pressed her cheek against Jack's and talked in a quiet voice. Jack fell to his knees and bawled, feeling no consolation. Lillian caressed his cheek, but the boy pried himself from her arms, crossed the room, and kicked the wooden door, cracking the lower panel.

"He wants everything I have!" Jack screamed. "And more. I'll have nothing."

"Please. Be generous. In a while we'll go out for a little walk. Franco can join us. Maybe Sonny, too."

Jack quieted a little. He had always liked Sonny, always seemed a little envious that he was Franco's father, not his own, and always enjoyed doing things with him, especially outdoor sports. When the two boys left for the game room, now tossing the toy between them in a friendly, cooperative way, Lillian and Sonny grinned at each other in relief. It was one of the last times he saw her smile, and he always remembered the fond way she stared at their sons as they left, the elegant toss of her hair as she turned to embrace him, urging him to lead them all gently, Maresciallos and Salvaggis, to carry on for friendship's sake.

From that day, from that moment, Sonny always said, Jack was the one person in the whole depressing mess — among Salvaggis and Maresciallos — who seemed to change for the better. Perhaps it was all that heavy male authority hanging over him now: Carmine, Anthony, even Sonny. More likely, he thought, it was Lillian, her soul guiding him through the darkness. Jack didn't disturb things anymore. He remained quiet, settled, rarely causing trouble. Gradually, *gradually*, people still like to say, he behaved as gently as a lamb.

5.

"I'm not blaming your mother. Your father was the difficult one," Sonny said.

He glanced out the window. Rain covered the glass, casting a gray, dripping reflection of light and shadow about the room. "Your mother was lovely, special. I owed a lot to her. All of us did. But she wanted to die, Jack, much as I hate to tell you that. Do you know what a martyr she was to the people at the club — to the women in this community?"

Jack shook his head. He put his hand on Sonny's kitchen table and stared at Margo with a glum look on his face. She said nothing to him. By this time, two days after the ceremony, Franco and Roseanna happily honeymooned in Italy. Jack and Margo had indeed decided to stay with Sonny: a substitution (and exasperation) he had provided gladly for the unhappy friend-turned-enemy down the road.

Anthony had left the wedding early, standing abruptly in the middle of a song Margo and Sonny danced to. Obviously fuming, he had stalked through the crowd to the central table, taken Franco's hand and, with what Sonny saw as a malevolent, envious glance toward him and Margo, dropped an envelope into Roseanna's white handbag, touching her forehead with his lips. He ambled down the long path among the flowering trees and walked through the gate, shaking hands and smiling brightly at the Balducci family but not saying a word to anyone else.

Later, Jack, oblivious, returned with Margo to the Maresciallo house and found locked doors. No note, no sign of anyone awake within. As so often in his adolescence, he drove back down the road a quarter of a mile to lift the knocker on Sonny's door and spend the night. Next afternoon with messy hair and ever so slight hangover, he visited his father at the quarry office, anxious to settle whatever problem he hadn't noticed the evening before. It was Margo, of course — and Sonny; no need to mention their evening dance. But, Jack argued, that was all harmless and inconsequential. Besides, he loved them both, truly.

"And your father?"

"I love you, too, Dad. You know that. But what can I do?"

"Leave his house," Anthony shouted bitterly. "And send her back where she belongs."

An hour of argument, another of cooling off. But then they argued again, this time agreeing to let it go, or attempt to. Jack and Margo moved in with Anthony for a short stay, yet the "vibes," as Jack described it then, felt so uncomfortable after just one night that he and Margo returned to Sonny's.

"What is it between you two?" he asked Sonny that evening. "I can't even mention your name to my dad. There's always something that grates him, but it's never clear. It's not just the business, your building. It's never been . . . for me . . ."

"Easy," Sonny said. "Or simple. No, it hasn't. And you're right. It's more than the business. It's more because of the way your mother died. He blamed you at first. Then, for obvious reasons, he blamed me. What was I supposed to do — save her? I was half way down the street. But he never blames himself, never himself, cold fish that he is. Lately he blames me all the time. . . . Guilt," Sonny added, shaking his head.

Jack glanced at Margo, frowning as if to confirm something, and then studied Sonny for a moment.

"What made him hate you? What started it, I mean. He always talks about jealousy when he talks about you."

Sonny shook his head, sighing.

"Was it really my mother, or something more? Carmine, my grandfather, maybe? You —"

"Carmine —" Sonny nodded. "Partly. He always liked me, too, you know, I think because my mother was alone. Sometimes he seemed to like me more than Anthony."

Jack nodded, remembering. "But there must have been something that started it." He turned, staring into Margo's eyes, then back to Sonny's. "Did you ever have anything to do with the same woman — like my mother — you know, romantically?"

"Well, hardly. Though your mother. . . ."

Sonny looked at Margo and shook his head.

"Were you romancing my mother on that day?"

Jack turned away from Sonny. He had no visual memory of his mother's death. He said that often, although he still remembered mumbled words, a sudden scream, as well as the muffled sound of the horse's hoofs and wheels pounding over her body. In the last image he held of her that day she was smiling and holding his hand as they walked down the street, toward something or someone.

Sonny shook his head, when Jack looked at him. "We had nothing besides friendship — deep friendship, I'll admit. Your mother smoothed out my rough edges. Oh, when we were young, there were a couple of girls your father and I both liked. One, Mary Ricardi — you knew her family in high school, I think. But . . ."

"But not my mother? You never had anything —? — You know, anything —"

Sonny stared at the table, solemnly. "Nothing. Nothing ever happened."

"Even on that day? I don't remember much, but you were there. I remember that."

"I used to talk to her — a lot. She was my friend. We visited when I brought Franco to play with you. You remember your father then, maybe. As miserable to her as he was to you. It was a bad time because he saw how much business I had. Anthony didn't like it, but there was never anything else."

Margo frowned, and Sonny noticed. She wore blue jeans, and a red and black plaid shirt, open at the neck. An Indian necklace of beads dangling between her breasts, obviously hanging unencumbered beneath her baggy shirt. Sonny felt himself drawn to them, found it difficult, for the silliest of reasons, to turn his full attention to Jack or his father.

"Why do you hate each other so much?" Jack said. "Let's be honest, why do you hate him?"

"Hate? — That's a little strong." Sonny shrugged, still staring at the beaded necklace. "But I have my reasons, as I suppose he has, too."

"Well, what the hell are they? It's about time he knew."

That was Margo, frowning. Sonny glanced out the window again and forced himself to turn to Jack.

"It's the way we've always been," he said. "Competitive, even as kids, never close like you and Franco. We both wanted Carmine's attention — and the town's. Now it's a lifelong habit that we haven't kicked."

"Town? — You mean the Garibaldi Club, don't you?"

Sonny nodded. "Mainly. A little business, a little character. Two old Italian-American geezers trying to fit in. I don't know. . . ."

A breeze blew. Shadows of leaves gave the drops on the window a ghostly blue hue. Sonny found himself studying them.

"Hell, I made a go of it," he said, staring back at Jack and then at

Margo, "on my own, I mean. I started with nothing. While Anthony inherited —"

"We know, we know," Jack said.

He frowned and turned to the window, also. Then he looked down at the floor, silent. Something, Sonny saw, something not completely right, or pleasing, colored Jack's expression. He remembered little of his early childhood, Sonny knew, yet because of the lapses of vision and the images of that one day, Jack was clearly intrigued with Sonny's version of the story.

"The poor man hasn't found his place in life," Jack said.

"Place? Jack, very few people do — especially people like us. But your father has — has always had — everything! Money; house; comfortable position in town and at the club; a father —"

"A father? — One who gave him pressure and expectations . . ."

Sonny waved, continuing the count on his fingers. "An established business. A lovely wife — whom he left to herself from the start, by the way, the ungrateful bastard. Jack, other men sweat or die for what your father had. Place or no place in life, most never get it. Why should he be unhappy?"

Jack and Margo shrugged, smiling together spontaneously. At first Sonny didn't understand their looks. But at that moment they both turned toward him, and immediately he felt like a clown or, worse, an old man completely out of his time. Sonny pounded his thigh as he gulped the wine, home-made, he had reminded them, and far better than Anthony's would have been. From time to time his own son, Franco, laughed at him that way, most recently at the wedding. It was one of the times recently he had heard it from someone he still thought of as a child, and he was damned if he was going to take it again — especially from a young woman.

"In certain ways, Jack," he said, "I know your father better than you do, and certainly for a longer time. There are things you'd never dream. . . ."

Jack laughed now loudly and bitterly. "Oh, I've dreamed them, Sonny. Believe me, I've dreamed, and thought, them — almost every day since that afternoon."

Angry, he shook his head.

"It's not just dreams," Margo said. "His father won't talk about this stuff — important, real life events. Like arguments with you, or the events around Jack's mother."

Sonny nodded, observing the sober determination in her eyes.

"Do you agree with him? About his father's silence, I mean, that it's crazy?"

Sonny looked at her and nodded again.

"Real events are not very pleasant," he said. "Maybe we —"

Jack pounded the table and cried out, uttering no sound but a terrible out-of-control bellow. Margo turned and held his arm; slowly, she put a finger to his lips, but with a look of real motherly concern. Masterful, Sonny thought. Even loving. Yet she would goad Jack, until she broke him, or made him endure the pain.

"There are things I *want* to know," Jack shouted. "Things I have a *right* to know — god damn it! I'm her son!"

"About your mother and father?"

Jack looked pained and nodded. "And other things."

"The quarry? — Forget it. Your father's letting it go to hell! He could sell it, but he won't let me buy it. I'd really like to make —"

Jack shook his head. "No, Sonny. Let go of all that rock and dirt. I want to know about people — my grandparents and parents. There's so much they held back about their lives and marriages. Why couldn't my father forget my mother after she died? Why didn't you, even though your wife —?"

"Why couldn't anyone? It was a tragedy — the worst thing that ever happened in this community. Some think Anthony forgot her *too* easily. Some people think your father —"

Jack shook his head. "I heard the man cry in his sleep for months — like a baby. He talked to her. 'Come back. I need you — and Papa!'" Jack shook his head. "All night. Then in the day he turned it all on me."

Sonny looked at the floor. He could not bring himself to say a word.

"Because of you?" Jack said. "A warped affair!"

"No! — I don't know the cause, and I don't want to!"

Margo barely held back a smile, yet when Sonny looked at her, she turned away.

"What was it between you and him? Something —"

"It wasn't me. He treated your mother the way he treated everyone else. We were all beneath him. *Cafone,* he called us. He doesn't even have a son to be a friend with anymore."

"Don't say that, Sonny! It's not true!"

Jack swooped down to the table at that, his head cradled in his left arm. Ashamed, or overcome, he hummed in a loud, sing-song moan, hammering the table with his huge right fist. Margo kneaded his shoulders and neck to soothe him and whispered in his ear. As Sonny watched her massaging him, he looked above Jack's bobbing head into her eyes, held them, and then, when she returned his nod, let them go. Despite himself and the awful, pathetic sight of Jack, he felt the urge to reach across the table.

"Jack," he said. "Pull yourself together."

Sonny clenched his fist and held it before Jack's eyes. Margo laughed, her fingernails tapping the table as she leaned over Jack. In an instant, her look turned on Sonny, with genuine intensity. "Oh, brother," she whispered, loud enough for him to hear, "we are dealing with Neanderthals around here."

Sonny glared. Margo reached out and touched Jack's forehead, running her fingers down his nose toward his mouth. She massaged his temples till he straightened, humming distractedly. He stared glumly, stupidly, at the table top. Suddenly, he turned and, mouth open, kissed Margo hungrily on the lips.

"I am not ignorant," Sonny said, letting his breath out after a moment. He glared at Margo. "I know the word Neanderthal. I am not college-educated, but I read, thanks to Jack's mother. And I have seen the world."

"World. . . . What do you make of it? — That's what counts. And reading: Have you learned anything from it?"

Margo almost spit out the question. The green of her eyes virtually glistened, Sonny saw: polished, glowing stones.

"I have a sense of honor," he said. "I would not risk ruining a neighbor's life — or marriage — for a few hours' pleasure." He nodded. "I admit I wouldn't weep about it either."

Margo looked up, wide-eyed.

"Jack, did you hear?"

"Even with my father involved?" Jack asked. "You're sure — even though you may have hated him, and —?"

Sonny nodded, soberly. "I wouldn't — especially with him — to deny him the cause for vengeance. And I would never, *never* do anything to hurt your mother. She was fine; too fine for a goddamn world where everyone, everyone good, must suffer."

They stared at him, the humor completely drained from their faces.

"You were out to give him a pair of horns," Margo said. "I hear it in your voice."

"I was not! — Anthony Maresciallo is —"

Jack kissed her again, stopping Sonny cold. He looked away, ashamed, watching in the window's reflection Margo massage Jack's shoulders again. Nothing was clear about their lives this day, not even Jack and his girlfriend, or the idea of her being a bone of contention between two old, desperate men. He turned for another sip of home-made wine.

As Margo stroked and kneaded Jack's shoulders and neck, Sonny looked over the rim of his glass and, without trying, imagined her in private moments, sometimes with an amorous, untroubled Jack, sometimes with a happy, balding man huffing and puffing in her bed. Not plausible, Sonny thought, for himself or anyone else his age.

And yet . . . He had truly felt it, briefly, while they danced to that loud music at Franco's wedding and during one or two short moments since . . .

"Your mother and I were close," he said, "despite your father. She was too good, especially for that prick — excuse me —." He looked at Margo — "That awful man she lived with."

Margo's eyes did not change. At the table, Jack still bobbed on his folded arms, his loose mane of dark hair brushing his shoulders as if it were another of Margo's hands. On impulse, Sonny moved to caress her arm. He reached across, past the fruit and wine glasses, and, despite his doubts, touched, then held, Margo's elbow: gently at first, squeezing as if it were a delicate peach or apple instead of her smooth, pale skin. Silently, but with a small, tense smile, she pulled away, and Sonny felt himself letting out his breath.

"Anthony's had his wild times, too," he said, "although I know it's hard to believe. Did he ever tell you any of them?"

"I never asked," Jack answered.

Sonny shook his head.

"Oh, I asked once, when I was young. But he told me to mind my business. Later, it never seemed appropriate. He put too much stock in good behavior — his own, but mostly mine."

Sonny laughed. "He was a secret sinner, like most of us. But especially with one woman."

Jack looked away.

"There are things you'd never . . ."

Jack turned his head back, frowning deeply now. He was interested, Sonny saw, maybe a little worried, too. But Margo looked extremely alert now, expectant even, and very eager.

"Tell us," Jack said. "What women?"

Sonny hesitated, his hands outspread.

"He's a big boy," Margo added. "He should know about his parents — and their preferences." She looked at Jack and clenched her fists. "Right, honey?"

Jack slumped to the table again.

"Not preferences," Sonny said. "This isn't about that."

"Just what's convenient?" Margo asked.

"Just what *I* think is proper to know," Sonny answered. "I'm the story teller."

Puttana, he thought. She would cut a man down, lock his balls inside his belly. Jack had fallen for his own destruction, and — Was it possible? — maybe Sonny would like to join him.

"Does the name Bettini mean anything to you?" he said at last. "Barbara Bettini?"

Jack shook his head.

"Barbara Bettini — a piece of braided *scamorce* your father once had interest in."

Jack shrugged, nonchalant, although in a moment he appeared under stress. Grimly, Margo stared at Sonny as if she knew the story already — every sordid detail.

"Also, did he ever tell you about my wife, Lina? About the interest he had in her — when you were a kid? Then, later, after you and Franco went to college?"

"Mrs. —"

"Let the man finish, Jack. This is a story you've wanted to hear as long as I've known you."

"No — I don't! *You* do!"

Jack stood abruptly, pushing the table away, almost upending it. He spun and dashed through the door into the yard as if he had to vomit.

The wind picked up, driving rain harder through the trees and against the windows. Margo followed Jack, but she stopped at the door and, instead of leaving, turned. Closing the door, she came to sit next to Sonny at the table.

"Tell me more," she whispered, sipping the last of the wine from his glass.

"Tell you? — What about Jack?" Sonny tried to hide his puzzlement.

Margo shook her head. "He needs to be alone. It hurts to find some-one you love is a heel, especially a parent."

Sonny stared into the stone-green sinkers and blinked. Tempting, he judged. Not hopeless either: Margo wanted to hear. A story about nasty fathers and sons might open interesting paths.

"This calls for another bottle," Sonny said. "Let me get one from the basement."

He felt her fingers tremble — yes, tremble on his arm. As he left the kitchen table and opened the cellar door, he sensed that she might follow him.

LINA

6.

Sonny's mother, Modestina, had been happy overseeing the inn he had bought and renovated for her. Expecting a large family, he and Lina bought land for themselves and built a large brick house just above the Maresciallos', on a lovely rolling hill, about ten acres with a pine forest, a stream, and a cool, green pond in the middle of it. Their boy, Franco, grew up healthy as well as handsome, and very early he showed a studious nature that seemed a sure prescription for the professions. A happy prospect yet, with the days passing easily and positively, Sonny sometimes felt uneasy. Having risen rapidly — first at the quarry owned by Jack's grandfather, Carmine, then with Lina's father — to management and then ownership of his own business and land, he had little more to strive for in his forties. But the very beginnings of his unhappiness grew out of those achievements.

Pearl Harbor occurred in early December, and Sonny grew more unsettled as the war developed, dissatisfied with himself, his parents' native country, and the world around him. Was his father, Giovanni, the man who had seduced and left his mother, in Italy now, perhaps suffering, struggling against the yoke of swastikas and brownshirts? Worse, was he a fervent Mussolini supporter, a fleshy, older man, happy that the trains ran on time, smiling and waving a pathetic flag as El Duce motored past with his right arm extended in an obscene salute? Sonny wondered. He had heard that hundreds of Italian-American immigrants had been taken from their homes and relocated — some in a camp near Harrisburg, others farther west in other states. Meanwhile their sons marched off to Europe and Asia to fight and die against the Axis troops. He worried about his mother, still unmarried, who had come to this country at the turn of the century and spoke little English. On impulse in early 1942, he tried to enlist in the American army or navy, only to be pronounced physically unfit to serve: age, flat feet, and right ear — the eardrum having burst years before from a dynamite explosion at the Maresciallo quarry. But, really, was it a lack of trust? He volunteered for civil defense work, and, to his surprise, was accepted. On certain days he envisioned his father striving somehow in poor health to keep up with columns of booted, robust German and Italian soldiers marching through the mud on the way to or from Rome, into or down from the dry mountains and loose boulders of Basilicata, where he knew his mother had been born.

At the Garibaldi Club most of the younger men had enlisted to fight by summer of that year, but among the older ones, like Sonny and Anthony, whose parents had arrived from Italy nearly half a century ago, mixed feelings reigned, especially with the American invasion of Europe. How could their innocent family relatives manage? Communists prodded them on one side, Mussolini and Hitler marched forces on the other. Should we, as good Americans, Sonny thought, be aggressors too, hacking at the very roots that once nourished our families? Yet, everyone — *everyone* — said that after Pearl Harbor, this war had to be fought. And won.

It was then, despite his mother's scornful laugh, that Sonny began searching for Giovanni in earnest, telegraphing officials and business acquaintances in central and southern Italy. Hardly anyone responded, a postcard with a guarded message arrived now and then, once an official letter denying knowledge of any specific Giovanni Franco Battaglia, which was the name Modestina gave him for his father. Few, if any, letters got through, and with the war on furiously now, after two years of trying, Sonny gave it up.

Perversely, he admitted to Jack once, he then began to seek direction elsewhere.

Women had always been easy for him, certainly easier than happiness and success through war efforts and tracing a lost father. He had time and money to spare. He had developed style, and to his surprise women found him attractive as he aged: fine wine mellows, they said, as do men. Driving about for business or some defense project in the mountains and surrounding small towns, Sonny met wives and daughters as unsure about their lives and futures as he. What were their men doing in France, England, Belgium? How were they responding to the island women of the Pacific? Or the WACs, WAVEs, and nurses assisting them? Would they return? Would they want to? If so, with what physical or mental damage?

He did not extend himself. As he assured Margo and Jack at a later time, Sonny never took advantage (never intended to) of other people's misfortune. But civil defense provided a perfect excuse for men and women to stay out late and, sometimes, not come home at all. Lina assured him that she understood, especially since, in Florida, her retired father, Tomaso, had taken up civil defense himself and wrote frequently about coming home well into the morning hours. But something happened to Lina during those sad years, an unnoticed, unacknowledged bit of war statistics. Isolated, confused by her two countries' war, a busy husband, and very distant parents, Lina spent long hours alone, drinking.

Sonny hardly noticed in the beginning. Embarrassed, he returned early in the morning, sometimes from volunteer work, sometimes from another woman, found Lina asleep with the blackout shades completely drawn and Franco's crib behind a screen in the corner of their room. Seeing nothing amiss, he kissed her tenderly on her lips and undressed. She murmured a sleepy "good-morning" as he slid beside her under the covers, and then, with her superb white arms draped about his neck, she would gradually arouse him and they would make love, half in their dreams, until they both drifted off.

At breakfast Lina acted absent-minded and tired while he read the war news, but her lovely smile and her jokes at her own expense ("I can't keep anything, including myself, on its feet today!") allowed Sonny to pass over a search for cause.

But as the war ended and they had more free time, her drinking grew more obvious and Sonny drifted farther away. Civil defense no longer loomed, and so the new excuse of increased business activity kept him away. At the Garibaldi Club or any place else in town, his private life held few secrets, and Lina's drinking became a prominent topic. To protect Franco Sonny took him to Lillian for most afternoons and occasional weekends. As fond of Jack as of Franco, Sonny thought both boys would profit from a friendship as they grew older. Jack had muscular grace and speed, encouraging Franco into team sports and other physical activities; meanwhile, Franco encouraged Jack to sit still and use his brain. Anthony raised a few objections after Lillian died, but he finally agreed to allow them more time together. Less than a year apart, they both entered the same grade since the elder Jack had started school late.

The two fathers alternated driving them to school, and Jack's grandmother, Carmella, brought them back to the Maresciallos in the afternoons. They played together in the house at the foot of the Maresciallo's Quarry until Sonny picked up Franco in the evening, calling occasionally to ask Lillian if his boy could spend the night. By that time Sonny would not trust them — alone or together — with Lina.

"Motherless," he told people. "Or as good as that."

He rarely apologized for his own behavior — to Franco, his mother, or anyone else — but more often than not he felt he should have. Salvaggi Enterprises, especially the construction arm, demanded more energy, and life at home had gradually become unbearable. By 1946, he no longer slept in the same bed with Lina, yet when he allowed himself, Sonny still felt love and found her attractive. Her hair shone beautifully dark when she was happy, and a warm, youthful glow still filled her eyes. She had lost that giddy, girlish humor he used to admire, but her smile, when she wasn't drunk, still held soulful hints of warmth and love.

Drunken mornings were cranky, difficult. Lina trudged through a gray fog that seemed to weigh on her shoulders, forcing a grim, burdened expression on her face. Wine, once a pleasant accompaniment to food or friendship, became a replacement for both, deepening the furrow of lines across her forehead and near her eyes. Even on her good days Sonny looked at them and turned away.

A woman across the river in New Jersey wanted him: thirty-five years old, a public school teacher. In winter 1948, they vacationed together in Italy (a voice teacher, she wanted to hear opera from its source while Sonny made another futile attempt to locate Giovanni Battaglia). Under the pretext of business, he also spent weekends with her in New York and Florida. Sonny liked her for many reasons, but mainly because she allowed him to understand quality by more than dollars and cents. Her ideas, her habits of mind, differed from any woman's he had ever known — except for Lillian Maresciallo, perhaps, and his mother.

"There are things a man must find in this life," he told Modestina, when she complained about his treatment of Lina and Franco. "Some find them in war or business. Some, like my father, Giovanni, have to experience them in other ways."

"Your father! You bring that bastard up to me?"

He nodded, looking straight into her eyes. "I'm sorry, Mama."

She waved. Tall, thin, turning rapidly arthritic, Modestina wore a white polka dot dress. She pounded the table fiercely, rattling silverware and teacups in their saucers before leaving the room.

"Study this," she said, returning quickly. "I received that in the mail — many years ago."

Sonny held it, trembling. An old sepia photograph, faded at the edges, bore the image of a man in his early fifties, dressed in a dark coat and hat. He wore a handkerchief around his neck and carried a smoking cigarette in his hand. A body of water, the Mediterranean, Sonny guessed, stretched out behind him to the horizon. He looked thick, thicker than Sonny had ever been, also more handsome and self-assured. Yet in the dark eyes beneath the curls on his forehead, Sonny read a message not so confident — and less clear.

"Giovanni? You knew where he was and never —? What address, Mama?"

"I *don't* have his address. I don't want it!" Modestina turned away in disgust.

Shaking, Sonny studied the picture carefully. "Mama, he was not good to you, or me. But he was a man."

"*Man!*" She spat the word back at him. "What is that? — A bastard, a coward, and a selfish one, too?"

Sonny winced. "Bastard," never sounded empty of meaning, but he went on. "There must have been something my father had to do before settling down. That's why he left us. But he sent you —"

"*Us. . . ,*" Modestina stared at Sonny, her frown carrying a lifetime of anger and defense.

"I have felt the same need in my life," Sonny said. "With my friend —"

"Your friend! You mean your *pu* —"

"Mama, my *friend* has helped me in ways Lina never could."

His mother closed her eyes. She would say nothing, but even she, Sonny knew, must have noticed the recent changes for the better. He dressed more appropriately now, and with flair. Beyond business, he read books and magazines. He learned about new, artistic things, and his pride in that knowledge sometimes beamed from his face. He saw it, and Modestina must have, too. But Sonny could not tell her the rest of the story: that the teacher was not Italian or Catholic; that as far as she was concerned the "friendship" must end soon, in one direction or another. And that to prevent her from seeing other men he had promised to live with her in another month, after he had arranged for Franco's — and Lina's — care.

"You are a disappointment," his mother said, "a tragedy. But I love you. I hope you will learn your lesson — a bigger one than these beautiful 'things' this woman teaches you."

Modestina rose, pulled the photograph from his hands and balled it up with a grand, fierce gesture before hurling it into the garbage. "This is where the *diavalo* belongs — especially after all these years."

Sonny pulled the balled-up photo from a pile of soggy tea leaves but did not respond. Modestina shouted, reminding him of the radiant young bride and mother that Lina had been, recalling their own former hardships when she had no husband for support. But she wounded him with special pain by referring to Franco as a boy without a father —"Just like you!" she cried. Motioning toward the wrinkled and moist photograph that Sonny had flattened on the table, she added, "You have spent your life chasing a . . . a *nothing*, expecting a miracle to make it real."

"Mama, I turned out fine. Can you deny that?"

She screamed. "You are perfect! A perfect father with his sick head in the clouds and an alcoholic wife at home."

"Mama . . ."

"Get it through your head, *figlio mio*. You are alone, responsible — *for yourself*. No father will recognize you — ever."

"Mama —"

"You have no father to claim! Believe it!"

Sonny gasped, hardly breathing. Light poured through the windows, creating a false, cheery brightness around them. Finally, Sonny said, "You know I've done well, Mama, with or without a father. There's no reason that Franco shouldn't either."

Modestina slapped his face, twice. Surprised, he fell back into his chair as she stood over him. The sting from her palm spread across his cheek and nose to the other side. His gums hurt, and his tongue might have been bleeding. He put his hand to his forehead.

"You call *this* all right?" she said, her hands spread toward him. "Betray your wife, let her become sick on drink, then, when you are through, find another, younger — a *puttana*? *La merda*! You have learned nothing from me . . . or her! *Stupido*!"

She slapped him again. And twice more. When Sonny raised his hands, Modestina lost control completely. Without stopping, she rained blows from both hands onto his head, shoulders, and back. Standing now, he stuffed the photograph in his pocket, covered his head, and stumbled across the room beneath her fists. He could hardly breathe. Still she ran after him, her fury seeming to grow until, with a mopstick high above her head, she stopped suddenly and fell back in her chair.

"*Diavolo*! — Like the one before you!" she sobbed.

"Mama, please! I am nearly fifty years old, a father myself. I help with the expenses of this house. I will send my son to the very best schools. I am not all bad."

Sonny stood, trembling, as far away from his mother and the mop-stick as he could. He heard her breathe heavily and for a few moments feared a collapse. Instead, she raised her hand and slammed it on the table.

"No!" She shouted. "No! You are not all bad. You are destroying yourself, your family, your wife. But these are small things."

He lowered his head, stepping toward her.

"Mama . . ."

"I don't want to hear! You might as well be a gangster — a killer — carry a gun! Money excuses it!"

She covered her ears as Sonny approached, lowering her forehead to the table and saying nothing. They remained still, silent, for a long time, only Modestina's heavy breathing interrupting the steady hum of steam from the corner radiator. Finally, calmly, she raised her head and put her hand on Sonny's.

"Think clearly, honestly, of *real* necessities. You cannot easily throw away these years."

"Mama —"

"And life is never new! You will find that out! Never!"

Sonny nodded, sobbing himself now, saying nothing more.

"Yet you will leave them. I know it. You will leave Lina and your son; you will regret everything! And I will, too!"

Sonny's stomach churned. He raised his hands to his ears and tried to stop her voice.

Modestina's hands covered his, squeezing his fingers. Approaching eighty, she still had surprising strength, and at that moment all her energy condensed into fists.

"I'm sorry, Mama. For everything."

"You should be."

"I will think about these things."

"You better."

But then she smiled, embracing him and kissing his reddened cheek. What more could he say? Looking at his watch, he went to a chair in the corner to retrieve his coat.

"Don't destroy us! *Don't destroy your family*!" Modestina screamed. "For what? — An untrustworthy, cowardly bastard — and this woman!"

"Please . . . I have enough to think about — already," Sonny said.

He turned and saw tears rolling from his mother's eyes. Running to her, he embraced her and fell to his knees before her. She shook her head, lifting him, and with her sobs and words ringing in his ears, he re-treated slowly through the door.

7.

He entered the quiet house, immediately noticing the rank odor of must, as if entering a cave, the earth, or a basement with no cement covering the soil. "Stench," Sonny thought, shaking his head. "Windows closed. She hasn't had the sense to put on the fans."

The dark living room, shades drawn, books, magazines, and news-papers uncharacteristically piled neatly on a corner table. Ashtrays emp-tied, teacups (usually three or four at a time, with varying amounts of whisky or rum in them) now gathered up, washed, were neatly arranged on the drying rack in the kitchen. Meanwhile, he could not fail to notice every bottle of rye, scotch, or gin lay empty in a sack in the kitchen closet. He spotted a note pinned to the brown paper bag: "To be thrown out," it said, in Lina's hand.

Despite the smell, the air seemed clear, unusually dust-free; rugs had been vacuumed, tables, chairs, lamps, and photographs had been wiped clean. Even the windows looked clean, along with the mirror above the phone on the table in the hallway and the one in the half-bath just off the kitchen. Their cleaning lady hadn't come of late because Lina had given her time off to visit a daughter at the other end of the state. Sonny had laughed when Lina said she would clean herself. Yet she had done it — and obviously in a first rate way.

He started up the stairs, wondering how to reward her, commend her. He thought of flowers and dinner out, a phone call to her parents or some distant cousins, perhaps an automobile ride to the Jersey shore. But as Sonny reached the second floor and turned on the light, another thought struck him: "She has left. After all these years, Lina has packed her things and gone to someone else. That —"

He thought of Anthony and then, in a panic of rage and fear, their son, Franco. But as he walked down the hall to Lina's room, Sonny reminded himself that neither Franco nor Anthony would suffice for Lina — else she would have left him long ago. He had gone for a week, to Italy, Basilicata, seeking traces of his father again. At last officials in Potenza had informed him that, according to their records at least, Giovanni Franco Battaglia, the man in his mother's photograph, was one of thirteen Giovanni Battaglias residing in that province since the turn of the century. But as far as they knew, none had ever traveled farther away than Rome.

Must lay heavily in the house, rich with a sweet sharpness that reminded Sonny of flowers, decayed ones. He recognized Lina's perfume, a scent he once had bought for her in France and that she had re-ordered through a jobber and worn continually for nearly twenty years. But there was another, unfamiliar, odor, distinctly sour and at the same time unforgettable. Sonny thought nothing of it, thought Lina had possibly vomited, or done something particularly shameful by mistake and left the house quickly rather than face up to him with its presence so evident in the air.

Smiling, he went to the thermostat in the hall, switched on the air circulator fan, and removed his jacket and hat. His postcard from Naples lay nearby, telling Lina about Amalfi and Vesuvius, informing her he would fly home shortly. With the jacket slung over his arm, Sonny went to Lina's room and opened the door: the odor, stronger here, stunned him, sending him reeling into the hall then, in memory, back to years when he worked for Carmine Maresciallo: the quarry workers had to cut through pockets of foul air in slate mines filled with gas or the stench of naturally decaying material. When his eyes focused in the dark of the room, he saw Lina on the bed, her face turned to the wall, her hands thrown out with her arms above her head and twisted, as if she had suddenly decided to defend herself. Everything else looked reposed, deliberate, and somehow the sense of purpose kept him quiet, made him cautious.

Lina's hair lay curled and combed; a candle, now out, smoldered on the night table; a single rose, dry now, rested near her shoulder. She wore the same dress, pale, cream-collared and lavender, that she had worn on the day they met, many years before. Sweat stains and other fluids, he imagined, darkened it here and there.

"Lina?" Sonny crossed the room at a measured pace to touch her, and, at the bed, felt what he already knew: cold. He saw that she did not breathe and noticed the expression of her face, absolutely, unreally, neutral, not terrified, not even sad. He wanted to scream, but instead he whispered her name again, not in anger or despair, but genuine surprise. At the end of her pillow Sonny found an envelope with his name scribbled on it in Lina's hand. He took it, disentangling it from one or two strands of her hair, and sat on a corner chair to read. Opening it, he saw another envelope inside the first: not addressed to him.

He stopped, looked at Lina again, closed his eyes. He opened them, turned over one or two pages of her letter, and then began to read:

"*Caro, caro* Sonny,

"I am sober. I haven't had a drink in four days, so I do this with a clear mind and the expectation that things can only improve.

"I'm sorry. I haven't done much right in my life with you, and I hope that at last with this one act — horrible though it will be — I can achieve something properly. Some of our friends may laugh to hear this, but I have always thought that the best thing I ever did was fall in love with you . . . and then Anthony. And I've always felt that apart from these twin loves things in my world have gone downhill. I am ashamed, but I hope my mother and father — left behind now in this sadly speedy journey — can find it in their hearts to forgive me, that over there sometime in the future, they can see me without shame. Still there are some things I must discuss:

"Franco. I see your love for him, Sonny dear. You have always been kind, and I know you will take care of him. That makes parting relatively easy. Hug him, love him. And, I beg you, don't turn him against me. I have sent him a note already, but please reassure him that leaving has nothing to do with him — or his recent absences.

"My drinking. I know this has driven me into a separate place. Silly that my one unwavering daily joy should come for the price of a bottle. There are words for it, but none of them mean anything to me now. I'm sorry.

"Anthony. I am *not* sorry about him. In the end you left me with nothing, you know, for days at a time no matter what the reason: business, family, ah, yes, I know, love and fun and pleasure. If there is any vindication in what I've done (my drinking and now, this aftermath) it is because to you, to you and even Anthony, *I* was less important than what I meant.

"Anthony was thoughtful, sometimes romantic, but, for your information, Sonny, often aloof and very concerned with his family's business — just like you. And your own obsession with the past, your father, and through the years, some very progressive, very attractive younger women — I've heard all the rumors about them — has driven you away. I hope that this dress, my rose, these two letters, and my quiet, private exit will somehow make me memorable to you both. It will be some measure of accomplishment and reward.

"Believe me: I leave out of hope — and love — free of terror and despair. Despite it all, I believe life can be very good. We have all been blessed to share it.

"Lina."

For about fifteen minutes Sonny sat in the chair, breathless, staring at the candle he had lit again, which, very slowly, and with a quiet, insistent hiss, burned next to the bed. He felt himself wanting to cry, but he could not bring tears to his eyes. Nothing came to his mind; nothing came to his tongue. He had heard Lina and Anthony had begun to see each other again, but not seriously. He had seen that Lina felt depressed when he left and a little distracted; he had assumed it was nothing more important than a few ounces more or less of alcohol.

Meanwhile, he admitted, he had his own obsessions.

"You fooled me," Sonny whispered, addressing Lina on the bed. "We started well, we got somewhere, but. . . ."

He stopped, feeling his chest heave in a sob. Then he held his breath and wiped a tear from his eye. "If you are not sorry, I can't be either," he whispered.

He left the room, phoned the police, and, without a word to anyone about them, tore up both of Lina's letters.

MARGO

8.

For several years after the wedding, Margo wrote to Sonny and Franco from time to time. It was a tender correspondence, made up of cards mostly and an occasional letter when Margo wanted to discuss important things with either of them. Sonny believed that she wrote to him instead of writing to a father, although some days he imagined other reasons.

"I've been slumming most of my life," she wrote, not joking, "and there are times with Jack when I feel I am slumming still." That from a farmhouse in Vermont; after it she added, "You have no idea of the depression he can put me into."

Maybe she is slumming with me too, Sonny thought, or worse, playing. But he did his best, responding to her letters quickly (providing, as often as he could, little images of his Pennsylvania life in words and stories). He gossiped about the Garibaldi crowd, especially the Maresciallos, and advised her about Jack and other men, pleased that he had won her trust about private matters. Much as Sonny liked Jack, he encouraged her to talk about her doubts and fears, saying that he understood them. Jack had a troubling character in many ways, a kind of emotional neutrality, as if he had been stressed inside and needed to block compassion. Although no longer the aggressive little boy his mother had to grapple with, he often made you worry. He might do something violent or crazy. Margo's complaints, Sonny said, might have real cause.

They had left Sonny's house two or three days after the wedding, returned to Anthony's, then driven north to New York State and east into Massachusetts. There they were directed farther north to Vermont by some friends from college, where they found an old farmhouse, owned by an art professor, that had a wood stove and no hot water. In the romance and necessity of their youth, they stayed because the professor let them have it for nothing that whole winter. They remained for three years.

Jack cleaned the attic and barn, chopped wood for heat and hot water, and skillfully remodeled the house, patching the roof, pointing the foundation, and applying a fresh coat of paint outside and inside. Margo dusted everything, sewed curtains, learned to cook on a cast iron stove, and canned vegetables and fruit that they found at stands on the road into town.

"Old fashioned but often fun," she wrote Sonny, and for Jack it remained one of the high points of their life together. "Tranquility," he
told Sonny. "The real thing."

While they worked hard on the house and grounds, they also found
time to read, camp, skate, and hike. Jack said Margo inspired him, providing ideas for "unusual constructions" of wood, stone, natural prod-
ucts, and debris he found in the surrounding forest or in the basement
and attic. Jack, Sonny gathered, had begun to fancy himself a sculptor
as well as a naturalist.

They made friends with people in a nearby town. Margo convinced
craft shops and small tourist museums to display Jack's carved and as-
sembled pieces, and he won a county-wide contest with one, earning
five-hundred dollars that they immediately put toward food, clothes,
and a night out in town. Dealers urged him to change his name to Jack
Marshall ("Pronounceable," one shop owner informed him. "Most people think Maresciallo is a piece of cheese."). He burned the new name
into the bottom of his sculptures, but after a year of little successes,
Margo said, other problems started.

"It's more than the times," Margo wrote to Sonny. "He's been on
edge for months." Jack had begun to talk, sometimes vaguely, sometimes compulsively, about a need for children, to build a family life.

Margo refused absolutely. They argued often, and in the fall they
moved to Boston where she began graduate work in French literature,
while Jack grudgingly supported them through masonry and other building
jobs. Making up for the move, she promoted his sculpture in Boston. Calling him an Italian-American Thoreau, she managed to place Jack's woodsy
pieces in one or two minor citywide shows. He turned out more pieces,
assembling leaves and scraps of paper, tree limbs, gathered from the park,
stripped of bark, and charred: but the work never caught on, despite its
environmental, outdoor qualities. Very few people bought it, except for
students. Critics hardly mentioned it, promoting the intrinsic, but denying
the aesthetic, value of his recycled assemblages. Jack continued his construction work to pay their bills, but he also began to drink and resented
the time Margo put into studying, as well as promoting him.

She went to the library for long hours daily. He began to socialize
with construction friends, and, in the mood of the times, also experi-
mented in various ways. When the art professor who had lent them the
Vermont house visited Boston during Margo's exam period, Jack went

out for an evening with him. As he related it in a call to Franco and Sonny several days later, he "found" himself in the professor's apartment "by accident" enjoying being fondled.

Fresh and still feeling virginal next morning, he refused an invitation to go out again the following night. They played tennis in the afternoon, and, as Jack said emphatically, "that was it — everything." Still, playing tennis changed something for him, and it began to take over his life. He met other, better players on the courts, and they helped him work on his game. Naturally graceful, he learned quickly. "Tennis, rather than art," he wrote to Sonny. "Sport rather than hanky-panky: motor skills and eye-hand coordination, with a lot less ambition."

He improved a great deal, apparently, competing with better and better opponents as the weeks passed, and he began to travel to different city parks and clubs for pick up matches.

"You'd have to see him on the court to appreciate it," Margo wrote in one of her letters. "Jack's found himself at last. In tennis whites, he cuts a wonderful figure."

Sonny doubted her story. He would not see Jack play until many years later at the Garibaldi Club, but once he did, he certainly understood. Jack's long hair, thinning already, but still dark and curly, hung down to his shoulders. His body, as in high school, possessed strength, speed, and effortless muscular control. "He's a ballet dancer with a racquet," some of the Garibaldi women said of him. Sonny nodded, seeing that age had conferred something new on Jack, and when he ran or leaped for an overhead or serve, spectators, especially women, could not divert their eyes. On Cambridge and Boston courts, with his strength undimmed and his dark hair not yet grayed or thin, Jack probably possessed even more charisma. "In another country, or another time," Margo wrote to Sonny, "he might have been a model, not a sculptor."

Meanwhile, she progressed rapidly in French, earning her master's degree, then teaching undergraduate courses as she worked toward her doctorate. They visited Montreal for the summer, and while there she received notice that she had won a grant to study in Paris the following winter. "The world is opening up," Jack said, hugging her, "and I'm sure this is just the beginning."

They returned to Pennsylvania to pack up Jack's winter clothes, visit people, and say good-bye. Reluctantly, Anthony gave them money, and after a Garibaldi Club farewell party, Franco and Sonny drove them to the airport in New York. Margo blushed with pride and happiness as they passed through check-in; Jack looked tired, a little scared, but also jubilant. It was more like a beginning than an ending, he told Sonny, especially for the life he thought he saw ahead of them.

9.

The boulevards grabbed them, along with the mansard roofs, and all the art museums. She attended classes at the Sorbonne; he sculpted in their room and painted canvases on an easel along the river. But within months Margo became pregnant —"unplanned," she assured Franco — and soon afterward decided to cross the Channel to London for a free, legal, abortion. Jack cried out bitterly, when she told him. Appealing to her better nature, he argued that a child might mature them (him especially, he admitted), provide a sense of purpose, and bring them closer together, especially in Paris.

"I can't think of anything better than being a father," Jack told her. "It's got to be challenging — and fun."

"Rot," she said, "especially when we're not ready. And you know it, Jack. I want more, much more, for both of us. We didn't come to Paris to start a family."

"You didn't," he said. "But who's to say this isn't part of a larger design?"

Shrugging, she laughed angrily at this fatalism and turned away. He peppered her with kind words and loving attention, solemnly promising he would care for the baby himself and let her go to classes. The stipend from Margo's scholarship would get them through the next year, and eventually he would find regular work to help with their expenses. Margo fought him at first, but gradually, whether from hormones, genes, or, as she thought of it, pure feminine stupidity, she gave in. "I let him change my mind," she told Franco. "Without intending to, he made me see another part of my life."

They took a train to the American Hospital in Neuilly late that summer and, a few days afterward, brought home a baby boy: "Marcello," Margo wrote, including a picture. "An absolutely beautiful little guy.

Even with the red tiles and chimneys of Paris rooftops all around us, his slightest gurgle amazes us, his face is lovelier than any sunrise I've ever seen. I know you won't like to hear this, Franco (and Sonny), but when we came home I said to myself, compulsively, 'My baby! Mine, not his!'"

Clearly charmed, Jack bragged about the strength of his son's arms and even approved of his loud cries and restlessness in the middle of the night. But something in addition to fatherhood filled his comments and his letters back home, amazing, yet worrying both Sonny and Franco: He trained with serious tennis players now, he told them, worked on tennis strategy with a professional coach, and began entering tournaments throughout the country. Within a year he received a national ranking in France. Playing daily for hours at the Luxembourg Gardens and other courts he became a tennis "semi-professional" as he called himself, giving lessons to make money for the family, winning a tournament every week or two, and, generally, thinking of himself as an athlete rather than an artist.

During winter nights he and several friends sneaked past a sleeping guard at the gate of a gymnasium at the Sorbonne, turned on the lights, pushed aside parallel bars, gym horses, and dangling rings, and played tennis on hardwood floors until long after midnight. "Don't see much of Margo and kid lately," he admitted in one of his letters. "My nights are full of racquets and balls; I'm beginning to see some light going on there."

He occasionally brought players home, men or women, introducing them to Margo and grinning self-consciously as they discussed matches rather than the child sleeping behind the screen near the dark armoire. She brought coffee in the morning, knocking on the studio door one flight up in the attic that he had cleaned out and taken over during the winter. She left a tray with two cups on it and a note reminding Jack that she had to leave for school soon; he would have to look after Marcello.

Rapidly, the boy — and Margo — took second place. Jack accepted invitations to clubs throughout France, especially in the south. Older, married women, invited him to dine at their tables, and eventually he stayed with them between matches. Good wine, swimming pools, tours through ancient vineyards pulled at him, along with, of course, lovely, warm bodies. More than thirty years later, back in Pennsylvania now, whenever Jack donates blood or takes an HIV test, he wonders if that part of his past will come to haunt him.

"The best time of my life," he wrote to Franco once, "and I really think I have a chance to excel in the sport!"

This was the mid-seventies. At the time tennis heroes in France were Borg, Vilas, and Nastase, good-looking players whose strong, athletic style combined with European grace to give them masculine elegance. With his mason's arms and back, distinctive dark hair tied in a ponytail, with a band around his forehead, Jack fit their mold quite beautifully. On the streets of the Left Bank at night, people often mistook him for Guillermo Vilas when he walked with a backpack and several tennis racquets slung over his shoulder. Most knew better, but some of the younger Parisians admired him anyhow, the women openly staring at him in ways that he never knew back home.

In cafes he talked of *terre battue* at the French Open, *le gazon* at Wimbledon, and men and women who listened bought him drinks. Flattered, he stopped working and sculpting completely, depending for money on Margo and whatever he picked up at odd times in matches or tennis lessons.

That summer Franco and Sonny visited the south of Italy together, and on the way home from Naples they stopped in Paris. Margo had flown to England for an appointment with Marcello's doctor. Jack remained behind, meeting them at Orly and escorting them into the city. At the Luxembourg Gardens they saw he had become an important fixture at the tennis courts, sitting in the shade of a chestnut tree with a beer in his hand as he talked to junior tennis players and passers-by. He remained until dark each day, he said, stopped on the way home for a drink at his favorite Montparnasse cafe, then started the long walk to the river, up Rue Saint-Denis to the Boulevard de Strasbourg. From there he mounted the hills to Montmartre and, at last, climbed five flights of steps to the apartment.

"A nice life," he told Franco and Sonny that afternoon. Smiling across a café table in Montparnasse, Jack raised a glass of beer in salute, but to Sonny and Franco his puffy eyes and vacant, tired expression looked worrisome.

"Jack," Sonny said, sipping an espresso as they stared at passers-by, "everything *seems* great, but a sensible man has to question it. Where are you going — really? Your mother wouldn't have liked this direction. Your father —." Jack laughed and waved his hand at that. But Sonny decided to make him listen: "I know I sound like him, but you're too old to do anything serious with tennis. And art? — How long can you continue without success? You need to make. . . ."

With a broad grin and only the slightest hint of doubt on his well-tanned face, Jack finished the sentence for him. "I know, a living. But I don't care about that because this is Paris, maybe my last chance at genuine youth." Without the slightest shame, he added, "I don't think anymore. At least I try not to. I just do more of the same and hope it lasts."

Franco glanced at Sonny, who returned his son's look with a frown.

"You know your grandfather didn't cross the ocean for this," Sonny said.

"I know, but I did," Jack replied. He smiled, though not with complete confidence, Sonny noted. "Sometimes I think my mother would understand."

Sonny shook his head. "You didn't know her, Jack."

"Well," Jack said, "but I've got her blood running in my veins. That gives me something."

For two winters her blood kept running — but wildly — as Jack took those long walks from the Sorbonne to Montmartre at night. In one or two of the cafes on Rue Saint-Denis, he played pinball and chatted with streetwalkers in for a rest between customers. He practiced French with them and, in return, taught practical, erotic phrases in English. He became close friends with a few, and once or twice, in exchange for cigarettes or a bit of marijuana, they invited Jack up to their rooms. He felt at home in Paris, Jack would tell Sonny years later. "In the world's most artistic city, I was a part of the people and its streets."

"But what about your family?" Sonny asked, remembering a similar set of questions from his mother.

Jack nodded ruefully, and they looked deeply into each other's eyes, acknowledging something equal and between them. As he had said before, it was a beginning of sorts, but also an ending, of everything he and Margo had once shared.

10.

At the Garibaldi Club in Pennsylvania some months later, when he talked to Sonny and others about his French experiences, Jack expected no sympathy from any of them and shrugged as if he didn't understand or care about his behavior with Margo. He mentioned separate interests and blocks of time doing different things: Margo visiting the library and lecture halls; he mostly on the courts or trying to paint and sculpt in his studio upstairs. Sport flourished, but art, along with his private life, became an absolute failure.

"It wasn't the university or Boston anymore," he said, referring to his work. "My stuff — sticks, stones, leafless tree-limbs, and sun-bleached soil — had no future in France — or, probably, anywhere else. Margo knows it. I'm an American, woodsy, a tree hugger. None of that seemed to matter in Paris. If I wanted to interest collectors or tourists, I had to do other things."

"And —?"

"I couldn't do it." He shrugged again, showing that empty, clueless, look that made Sonny want to shake him. "Honestly, I don't know why."

Practical club members (especially Sonny) suspected other, more serious reasons: motivation, choice, an unwillingness to take on responsibility with wife and child. Margo returned to the United States in the spring of 1980, and Jack followed her, reluctantly, after more than six months of sulking in Paris. "It was not a good time," he told people afterward, calling these months alone one of the worst periods in his life. He stopped playing tennis but indulged the boulevards often, drinking a lot, putting himself to sleep at night on a combination of women, drugs, and alcohol. Margo, disgusted but not surprised, heard about him from mutual friends. After finding a job in the city, she rented a one-bedroom apartment on the Upper West Side and began a new life with Marcello. Still, when a wrung-out and exhausted Jack, finally knocked on her door late one October evening nearly a year later, she agreed to let him stay temporarily.

"We're just friends while you're here," she told him, holding him at arms' length, "nothing more." She pointedly avoided his touch if he came near, although she smiled at Marcello's obvious joy with his father and encouraged Jack to do things with him nightly after school.

Relieved, Margo looked for a clearer sense of direction for the three of them, if only for Marcello's sake, and when Jack moved into a one-room studio near West End Avenue, not far from her apartment, she began to feel some hope. He bought a mattress, built a loft bed, found used chairs and a wooden table at the Salvation Army, and then arranged his life to spend as little time as possible among them.

For a year and a half Jack jogged in Central Park during the day, watched Marcello after school, and worked at night doing art and paste up for a weekly newspaper in lower Manhattan. He had stopped drinking completely now, proving to himself and Margo that he could change for the better. He saw the boy on weekends when she didn't take him out of the city, and they spent two hours each afternoon taking long walks to the Central Park Zoo and Fifth Avenue museums.

Seven now, Marcello had strong muscles and obviously good eye-hand coordination, so Jack taught him to draw and play tennis right away. He shaved and reshaped a racquet handle for Marcello's small hands, and during the dark winter months brought the boy to the Bronx to play in a tennis bubble managed by a friend. In warmer weather, they played in Central Park or on the clay courts beside the Hudson in Riverside Park. "Your influence," Jack said when Margo smiled at all that activity.

Once or twice she joined them on the court. Having played in college, she still had court presence, and Jack saw that Margo still showed the competitive drive of her college days. They practiced regularly with Marcello, played mixed doubles against the better neighborhood teams, and the following year played two or three weekend city tournaments, winning one. A couple of times Jack invited Margo out to dinner after playing, and one Sunday evening when her latest male "friend" had taken Marcello for a night out and a meeting with his family, Jack brought her back to his studio. After a few drinks, she agreed to stay awhile and, feeling optimistic now, he came close, very close, as he later admitted, to asking Margo to spend the night.

"Pitiful," Sonny thought, without saying it. He pictured Jack's little apartment as he had seen it once, its uninspiring view of an airshaft, the creaking elevator just outside the door, but he could only remember the passion, or at least the memory of it, weighing on that homemade bed. Margo left early that evening, and just a week and a half later, when Jack invited her up again, she asked him to come to her apartment instead — for "an important talk." In hindsight, Jack told Sonny later, he should have guessed he would not like the subject.

They had not talked at all, in person or on the phone, since that last meeting. What's more, she had seen her "friend" every night for dinner,

Margo told him. His name was Max, a lawyer who seemed to take a genuine liking to Marcello and, apparently, adored Margo shamelessly. They traveled together often, shared a series of opera tickets at the Met, and spent weekends alone at his private home near Philadelphia. But for Jack, although the direct signs from Margo lacked promise, unimportant events provided hope for something good: his mood, fine spring weather, Margo's warm friendliness a few weeks before, plus his own renewed eagerness about her.

"I'm just ready," he told Sonny and Franco on a visit home the week before he met her. "I've worked to clean up my act, but always with the goal of winning her back. I'm very susceptible to her love."

And the signs, the minor ones, proved good when he walked to her apartment. A cool, brisk wind blew off the river as he strode along a sunny Broadway sidewalk to see her. On impulse around 96th Street, he bought several bunches of daffodils and violets from a corner vendor and, holding them against his chest, he virtually floated up to her apartment in the elevator, pushing them toward her when she opened the apartment door.

"A first romantic gift," he said to her.

Margo paled, shaking her head for a confused moment as she took them, then stepped back and, with a wan smile, let Jack into the apartment. Arranging the flowers in a vase, she set them on a portable TV, and, very businesslike, retreated to the kitchen.

"Coffee?" she asked.

"Yes," he said, smiling. But it was then he saw the roses, probably two dozen of them, arranged on the windowsill near the stove.

"Lovely," he said, motioning toward them as she made the coffee.

Margo nodded. "I've always loved roses. They're always very special."

He said nothing. Margo wore blue that day — her best color, he said — denim shirt, faded jeans, milky blue turquoise dangling from her ears. Her bright red hair streamed down her back in a way he always found attractive.

"They're from Max," Margo said finally, her smile changing a little.

"I guess I figured as much," he said.

"And that's why I wanted to talk to you."

"Hmmm . . . I see."

He nodded, gravely.

"Things have happened lately," she continued.

"Apparently. . . . Lots of things."

He watched her grind beans, pour hot water through the filter, and carry the coffee pot, milk, and sugar into the living room on a tray.

She seemed neater, more in control than Jack remembered, and he tried to see through her quiet expression to something else, something more fragile. He surmised that a decision had been reached, and although he worked to preserve his earlier optimism, the message of her face and body shook him to the core. She poured coffee, offered milk and sugar, and in a blunt, flat tone, delivered her little speech: She had applied, been accepted to, and *would attend*, Margo firmly told him, the University of Pennsylvania in Philadelphia next fall.

"I'm very happy for you," he said, after a moment. "That's great." Despite his doubts, he added, "I'll try to move down there as soon as I can."

She held up her hand. "There's more." Margo frowned, as he nodded, obviously having difficulty telling him. "Just before that," she said, "Max and I intend to honeymoon in Europe and then live together — permanently — in his family home."

"Married, in other words. That's what you mean?"

She nodded. "And live outside Philly, just a train ride from here."

Jack held his breath. Margo added coffee to the barely touched cups. Sun, the no longer good sign, lit the room, bunching in a glittering patch beside Margo's slippered feet. He would remember looking for a moment at the view from her window — river, sky, the glistening George Washington Bridge near the Palisades and, what? — he would never be able to describe it — he felt himself go limp with absolute helplessness and disbelief, just as he had (and he was very conscious of this memory rising suddenly, he said) watching his mother lie on the pavement with Sonny and others gathering around.

He started to tremble and sweat, even as he looked at Margo's face and felt himself working to smile.

"I'm sorry," she said, rising, placing the coffee pot on the tray, and stepping toward him. "I didn't know how else to tell you. We've had a long, important time together, but now. . . ."

She paused beside him, taking the cup from his hand. For a full minute, Jack would remember, he could not let his hand drop.

Finally, steadying himself on the back of an armchair, he rubbed his hands but could barely make his fingers feel, much less warm.

"M — M —?"

He mumbled, sensing the icy moisture collecting in his palms.

"Max," she said, putting down his cup. "I've told you his name is Max."

"Yes." He smiled despite himself. Then, more quietly: "And you're moving. . . ."

"To Pennsylvania, yes. It will be difficult, of course, especially along with Europe and Marcello, but —"

"Marcello —!"

She smiled herself now, but with absolute determination. "Marcello loves Max. He'll be very content with us, and in Pennsylvania we'll be able to enroll him in a very good private school not far from the house."

"M — M — M —" Jack was not able to complete the sound.

He felt his arm tremble again and, trying to sort things out, took one of Margo's cigarettes. He lit it, smoking for the first time in four or five years and acting, as he described himself later, precisely like a movie clown, puffing in and out non-stop while folding and unfolding his hands. Still, he could not express his anger. He could not find a way. He looked into Margo's eyes, saw their cool, certain expression, and wondered if she had thought about his preferences. But of course she had.

"The city just isn't the place to raise a child," she said. "A more rural life outside Philadelphia will be good for him."

He nodded, blankly. He couldn't frown; he had no control of his muscles and couldn't do or say anything, good or bad, even later when he told Sonny and others about the meeting. Finally, mashing the cigarette in an ashtray, he looked at her and, when she smiled again, could no longer block his anger.

"Brainless Jack, the clueless jock, as everyone thinks of me. But there's another side to it: Does Marcello know he'll be far away from his father?"

Margo looked away. She turned her back, and then her frown softened as she returned to him. "Marcello loves you, Jack. We all know that. And it makes me happy when you're together. But you discovered him only recently, remember — here in New York."

He looked up from his feet, his arm shaking again as he spoke her name: "Margo, I love that boy. It took me a while, I admit, but I wanted him more than you. I love him — almost as much as I. . . ."

She raised her hand, stopping him. Bewildered, Jack shook his head.

"I still have some rights, you know. I'll defend them."

"We'll see," was all she answered, turning away.

"I want to see my boy regularly. In case you forget, I also think he should live with me from time to time. Weekends — summer. School vacations."

Margo stopped, looking into the galley kitchen toward the window and the roses. Taking that as a sign of weakness, Jack pounded his fist into his palm for emphasis. Across the street, he saw a young woman, leafing through a newspaper, sit up and stare at them, seemingly from the sound of his fist and hand. Meanwhile, in the apartment above her he noticed an elderly man leaning from his window, as if to look for something below. Fifteen years since they left college, yet to Jack it seemed he could turn, walk a few steps and observe a young, red-headed woman in a torn shirt pulling books from the stacks of their library shelves. He rose and walked to the window. Not turning, he shouted, "I'll get a lawyer, Margo. If I have to, I'll go to the goddamn police."

He thought he heard her sob, but then he realized the sound might have come from his own chest. He could clearly see, he remembered later, first her body then his own, hurtling out that window as they grappled with each other for control. Holding in his anger, he tried to imagine life, their lives, without something to share between them. "I *want* Marcello," Jack said to her. "I don't want him — or you — out of my sight."

She lowered the shade in front of him.

"Max has studied this carefully, Jack. You have very few rights; in fact, almost none. We've never married; you haven't supported Marcello for years, and you have very little money to support him now. With your history in France — which I would bring up if I had to, by the way — no judge or jury will make me keep Marcello near you."

She spoke cordially but firmly. Looking at the roses again, Jack imagined her hand upraised, reaching for his throat.

"I want you to know you can visit him when you want. And, of course, we'll bring him into the city from time to time. I want Marcello to be happy, and you —"

Whirling, he was surprised to see tears rolling from her eyes when he looked at her. She held up her hands. He started toward her anyhow, then forced himself, trembling, to pause.

"I want him here, in New York — definitely. All the time."

She lowered her hands and, with a grim, pale face, started toward the hallway closet. Opening the door, she pulled out an envelope, removed some photographs, and shook them in his direction. "Here," Margo said, "what you were — and did, so stupidly — in Paris. You and your friends."

He cringed, looking away, and his hands, no longer shaking, sweated from heat.

"Right here," she said, "everything I had to put up with. Women, a couple of men, the trouble you had with drugs in that whorehouse. I don't want to have to think of it again. None of it."

He could not move; looking at his palms, callused and red from hours of gripping tennis racquets and hammers, Jack wished he could simply make himself, at least that part of him, disappear.

"We're trying to be flexible," Margo said. "But the move is very important to Max and me. If you're not satisfied, see a lawyer. Have him contact us."

"Margo, why —"

"That's all I can tell you," she said. "That's all I'll say."

She dropped the photographs into the envelope and put them in the closet again. He crossed the room, stopped before her; she turned, and he raised both his arms in confusion, as if to embrace her. For a short, very difficult moment, he took her shoulders and shook her instead.

MARCELLO

11.

"He still feels ashamed," Margo wrote to Sonny a short while later. "And after all these months and years. Sure, I gave him hell. Any woman would have after what he put me through. 'You let us down!' I shouted, 'especially in Paris. And then you let us leave — eagerly!' 'If that's what floats your boat,' he said (Marcello will repeat it, I'm sure), 'I'll catch up with you eventually.'"

Jack had hardly spoken to her (or Marcello, for that matter) since that terrible spring day in her West Side apartment. When he thought of his son and former lover living out of easy reach, he wanted to erase the past ten years: every day of them. Instead, he dived back in again, retreating into heavy drinking, moving from one menial New York job to another, night watchman, clerk, handyman, even a walker of dogs, until one morning he looked at himself in a mirror, and decided he had endured enough.

That after more than two years without them. He hardly saw anyone from Pennsylvania during this time. Once in a while, Franco and Sonny Salvaggi visited; occasionally, he rode the commuter bus into the Poconos and passed a horrible couple of days arguing with his father and almost anyone he met at the Garibaldi Club. No one, not even his private self, approved of him.

They — and he — all considered Jack a failure, and out of pride or, perhaps, real denial, he had never bothered to take down Margo's new address and phone number in Bucks County. He had never made certain of agreed on times to visit Marcello or meet with him in New York. Overwhelmed by Margo's marriage and retreat to the country, he simply could not think about practical things, so much from desperation. He had no idea of the town they had moved to, or if they still lived in Max's family home, although he assumed they had settled somewhere near the university in Philadelphia. He asked Sonny and Franco about it, but they, out of a promise of silence to Margo, claimed to know nothing.

Following her wedding, several brooding, horrible summers followed. Jack started and stopped drinking again, returned to Smithfield to mend fences with Anthony, but only partly succeeded. He retreated to New York, renewed his layout job with the downtown weekly, and worked hard at not falling apart: private therapy, addiction meetings, one short, vigorous attempt at religion. He spent time with several women, one of whom had a boy Marcello's age, but each only brought about continual sadness. In the end, the plain, ageless desire to be with his child again kept him going.

He rode buses into New Hope one or two weekends a month and hitch-hiked, bicycled, or jogged on the country roads and highways around and outside town. He searched for Margo and Marcello, or at least signs of them, everywhere he went. Sometimes he traveled back home, borrowed Sonny's or Franco's car, and drove down to tour the Philadelphia area more quickly. He looked for "Hammel," Max's family name, in the phone book, on roadside mailboxes, and above or beside the doorways of stone and wooden country houses he pulled up to. Nothing showed, not even in the lawyer listings in the yellow pages.

The police gave him no information. At times he realized, because of the years and, more likely, his past bouts with alcohol, he could no longer put a clear image to Marcello's or Margo's face. If he saw a light-haired woman of a certain height on a lawn, or a couple of young boys walking along a country road, he would slow down, study faces, and then, almost frightened of recognition, step on the gas or pedals and move on past. He was sure he spotted Margo once or twice on the road into New Hope, but the woman, whoever she happened to be, drove too fast for him to catch up.

Quick glances in the mirror told Jack something more disturbing. He, too, had changed — not for the better. Though not drinking, he looked worn down and unhappy, as if some magnificent failure ate away at his soul and flesh. He had let his beard grow, and his hair, once dark and curly, had recently (and all too quickly) turned gray and thin. His appearance shocked his father, Anthony, at their first meeting. Muscular forms still bulked his arms, but Jack's neck and face, as if on another body, seemed to have lost some important strength. His eyes carried meaning, not emptiness, now, but it was a message layered over with shadow and loss. He looked tired, fearful, even thin, images his father and his other friends knew only too well from their own experiences in the mirror. If Margo or Marcello had bumped into Jack, Sonny told him, they might not recognize him — at least at first.

But Jack's inner stubbornness made up for the loss of strength and served him well. After searching through southeastern Pennsylvania communities for months on end, one Sunday afternoon he stopped in a small craft shop in New Hope to buy some drawing paper. There, wondering if he ought to give up the search and attempt some serious art again, he suddenly heard a voice — dim and high-pitched at first, then unmistakable in its tone and cadence. It made him hold his breath.

"Donny, I want to stop here. I need to get some colored sheets."

At first Jack thought he must be dreaming: the high voice, faint at the beginning, seemed to come from somewhere deep inside his head. But then, suddenly, it grew loud, boisterous — bursting into the shop, the door flying open with a sharp crack against a protruding counter and a jangle of its bell. Two boys jostled against each other while a dark-haired woman, pulling a dog on a leash, stopped and waited for them on the sidewalk. One boy looked exactly like Marcello — or what Marcello must look like, Jack thought, after several years. Slim but thick-armed, he looked about ten and carried a brusque, familiar restlessness, especially in his hands. He wore blue jeans, sported a shock of thick brown hair with cowlicks shimmering on top, and, glancing at Jack for a moment, squinted green eyes into the same inquiring slant that Margo had.

"Donny, do you want some of this stuff, too?" he called over his shoulder, louder than he needed, Jack thought.

"Nah, I have plenty at home. My Mom brings it from the office all the time."

The boy with the cowlick handled some brushes, sized up an easel, fondled a bag of clay, and, with a familiar, antsy sense of propriety, studied the sculpting tools near Jack. He shook his head when the dark-haired woman, apparently the other boy's mother, hooked the dog's leash onto the door handle and stepped into the store to hurry them up.

"Do you need anything more than paper?" she asked, not referring to the boy by name.

"No, this is it, Mrs. Borden."

"Then purchase it. I have a meeting, and I'm in a hurry."

With a glance over his shoulder, the boy took out some cash, stuffed a drawing pencil into his jacket pocket, paid for the paper, and, looking sideways at this bearded man with a grim, puzzled smile on his face, followed the second boy and his mother out the door.

Less than five seconds later, Jack darted to the sidewalk, turning side to side to look in all directions, but did not see them on the street. He searched the nearby shops, eventually walking to the tourist parking lots outside of town. Wondering if he had been in fact dreaming, Jack brooded at the station all afternoon and, on the bus to Manhattan that night, decided to change his tactics. The job in New York carried no importance; Marcello did. He gave notice at work again, sublet his share of the apartment to a co-worker, and paid off most of his New York City debts. Within two weeks he carried a couple of bags into Penn Station, bought a one-way ticket, and boarded a train for Philadelphia.

In New Hope, he bought a ten-speed bicycle and rode it constantly, searching in shops, cars, and schoolyards. He went to the police station again but, as much as he insisted, they saw his shoes, his jeans, his longish hair and beard, and told him nothing. He rented a small two-room gardener's cottage by a cornfield just outside of New Hope, took a job as a sales clerk in the very shop where he had seen (he hoped) Marcello, and kept his eyes and ears open. Finally, about three months later, his luck began to change.

As he rode his bicycle home for lunch one afternoon, Jack spotted Max Hammel's huge mane of white hair unmistakably shining above the wheel of a gray Lincoln Continental that passed him along the back roads near his house. Jack slid to a stop, changed direction, and, following without hesitation, caught up as the car turned into a small shale-covered road that wound along the opposite end of the cornfield behind his cottage. He pedaled hard, inhaling road dust all the way, amazed to discover Marcello and Margo might live so close, especially after the Continental turned off the shale-covered road for a dirt path among some tall maple trees. Jack had walked and cycled here several times already, the last just a week or ten days before. Three or four huge houses stood on the road, each on a lot of several acres, and at the far end nothing but hardwood and brush. The Continental stopped near the last house (no name appeared on the mailbox), garage doors opened automatically, and the man looking like Max Hammel pulled in.

Jack noted the huge house, an impressive three stories of tan stone and brick with a circle drive in front of it. "Everything," as he told people afterward, "proclaimed money — real, old money."

Topped by a wrought iron weather-vein, it had a slate roof, corbelled overhangs, and large wooden shutters, recently painted a modest Williamsburg blue. A gazebo stood at the back; in the garden behind it, off to the side near the woods, Jack saw a woman on a reclining chair.

She wore yellow shorts and a blue bikini top pulled low on her breasts. She lay on her back, reading, and as soon as he saw her bright red hair pillowed beneath her head, he knew.

"Not many changes," Jack told Sonny and Franco, as he tried with a few smiles here and there, to cover his eagerness. "Thinner in the face maybe; just a couple of strands of unbleached gray. But she looked trim, athletic — especially her arms and legs. It was very hard not to call out and say hello."

He left his bike in a clump of bushes about a hundred feet from the gazebo and walked carefully, tree to tree, until he stood ten yards or so to the rear of Margo's chair. He hid behind a gathering of honeysuckle and, like a nature lover admiring wildlife, studied her while trying not to move or make a disturbing sound. She wore a dark visor and lay beside a pile of six or seven books on the grass. He did not see or hear Marcello, and so he worked his way toward another clump of honeysuckle to view a part of the yard beyond the gazebo. He heard the back door click open, a few footsteps on gravel, and then he saw Max Hammel walking across the lawn. He looked happy, a good fifteen years older than Jack, but still in shape and obviously a man to be envied.

"A letter, my love — from number one son."

He chuckled. Smiling and kissing her, Max waved an envelope in his hand.

"Finally." Hastily, Margo leaned toward him and extended her arm.

"It must have rained."

She laughed. Max kissed her again and, with a squeeze of her bare shoulder and arm, handed over the envelope. Margo whispered something, laughed, and kissed his forehead. As Jack maneuvered behind a more dense bush, she tore open the envelope with her fingernail and read, chewing her lips and worrying the hair around her temple. Finally, she handed the letter back to Max.

"He seems happy at least. Thank God. I think it's good for him to be with other kids. I just hope he gets along."

"It will be even better when school starts this September. You'll see. They'll work him. He needs something to occupy his mind."

Max took the letter and started to read it himself.

"Whatever they do, I want him to be happy. He's had such a hard time."

Max looked up. "Don't worry, my love. It's a phase. He was bottled up when he first came here. That, too, will pass."

She nodded.

"It's a good camp. As you can tell from this, there was no real cause for concern."

Margo nodded again, this time taking Max's hand. "I want him to have a happy life," she whispered. "You've helped, but he deserves even more."

Max nodded. "Don't we all."

He smiled and placed his hand on her knee. Margo rested one hand on his and, with the other, adjusted her bikini top. The intimacy at such close quarters made Jack uncomfortable. But it worsened when Max moved his hand from Margo's knee and, with a sad, pleading smile of desire, slid it up her thigh. Her shorts were brief; she squirmed and stretched her legs as he touched them, resting her head on the chair back and studying the sky.

"What a day — perfect!" she said, as Jack, blushing, burned.

"For love," Max said.

He squeezed her thigh and, cupping the flesh, kissed her yet again. Laying the letter at her feet, Max pressed her breast and added, "I'm horny, Sweet. What do you think? — Do you want to go inside? You know, later —"

"Mmmm."

She wriggled and stretched some more, with Max looking serious and tender. The mournful expression of his eyes must have startled her. As if to acknowledge it, Margo sat up and kissed Max in a matronly way. Leaning forward, she cradled his head, holding it to her breasts. He squeezed her hand and murmured, "If I have it, or can get it, Margo, whatever it is, it's yours. Just don't give up on us. I couldn't stand it."

"Max, I have everything I could possibly want with you — you know that!"

They kissed again. Max slid next to her, pulling her onto his lap, and Jack turned away, listening until he heard their chairs move and saw them start toward the house. Margo's halter-top dangled from one hand. She looked young, girlish, her dark nipples shimmering like a pair of black-eyed Susans in a summer breeze. Beside her, Max looked rugged and content. As they walked up the steps to the house, Jack retrieved his bike, and, resisting the urge to peer through windows, slipped back into the woods.

12.

He decided not to return to the house until September because he reasoned that Marcello probably would be away until then. But he researched bus routes and discovered that the main one between New Hope and Greenleaf, a prominent outlying private school, passed along the very road where he had first seen Max. He called its headmaster, pretending to be Marcello's guardian, and learned the opening date of classes. The Greenleaf bus, the headmaster's secretary told him, stopped near the Hammel home on an unnamed road turning along the edge of a cornfield and pond. It became Jack's dream spot for the summer. He passed it each day, more and more slowly, as he bicycled to work.

He had trimmed his hair, shaved, begun to eat better, keeping away from alcohol except for an occasional can of beer. He planned to talk to Marcello the first day he saw him step off the bus, and he tried to imagine what they could, or should, talk about, never getting much beyond the formal handshake and hello.

Toward the end of August Jack could hardly control his eagerness and dread. On one visit to the Garibaldi Club, he told Sonny and Franco that his love for the boy was so wrapped up with shame that he felt sure he wouldn't be able to utter a word when he finally met him. Schoolmates might surround him; worse, Margo or Max. In any of those situations, he had decided, he simply would slip away.

As the nights lengthened, he found it harder to resist more than one beer, and as in his desperate New York days, Jack exercised to replace it. He biked, ran, and swam, traveling up to the Poconos occasionally to hit tennis balls with some of the younger players at the Garibaldi Club. By Labor Day weekend he could hardly keep his hands from shaking and felt grateful to work through the holiday at the store. Before work on Friday morning, he bicycled down the dirt road toward Max's house only to find the backyard empty, the Continental out of the garage, and neither Marcello or Margo in sight.

He glanced through first floor windows, finding no signs of anyone there. He noticed neat, clean antique furniture, Margo's familiar collection of French trade paperbacks on the dining room wall, and one of those tiled Scandinavian wood stoves on a slab of slate in the family room. But he saw no bats, balls, or toys, nothing with the messiness of a boy.

He returned on Sunday and found everything the same. Late on Monday night, as he passed again, exhausted after twelve hours of helping shoppers at the store, Jack saw lights shining from the windows. Curious, he rode right up to the house, picked his way through bushes to the back, and arrived at a safe first-floor window in time to see Marcello, the boy in the craft shop for sure now, cowlick quivering above his blue and white pajamas, kiss Margo, then Max, and finally run upstairs, with both their eyes following.

Strangely, Jack recalled his own mother, Lillian. Returning to his cabin at the other end of the cornfield, he slept badly that night and two or three nights afterward, though he made sure to return to the bus stop after work the following Monday afternoon. There, he decided to let his heart guide him in the meeting and, despite his resolve to leave if Marcello's friends or Margo accompanied him, Jack forced his legs and eyes to stand and watch.

He saw four boys leave the bus that day, each wearing a private school outfit — blazer, green tie, gray slacks, and a green and yellow cap on his head. Two of them carried satchels, one had a pair of manila envelopes and several books, and the fourth, Marcello, carried a red knapsack on his back. He stopped when he left the bus and squinted inquisitively in Jack's direction: that strange, familiar-looking man on a bicycle just across the street.

"Hey, March, come on, get over here! This is the way home — not over there."

"Let's cut through the woods. It's faster!"

"What are you talking about, faster? You haven't given one right answer to anything all day long."

"I'll answer you, you nerd, you shit!"

The four darted down the shale road — Marcello chasing the others and laughing — their heels kicking up gray dust and stones.

Frozen to his spot and not knowing what to do, Jack held on to his handlebars and watched, saying nothing. Down the road, the boys stopped, argued, lined up, shoved one another once or twice, and on a shout of go from one of them, abruptly raced to one of the trees about fifty yards away. They rested, then argued again. Marcello waved his arms and pointed farther on. With a shout they lined up once more and ran another fifty yards to a dirt path. Having won the first heat, Marcello just lost the second by a step.

Teasing each other, the boys lined up for a third try when something distracted them and, pushing and shoving as they went, they charged, squealing, cursing, giggling, deeper into the trees. Loud cries and muffled laughter filled the air. Jack saw a car, a white hatchback heading toward him. It skidded to a stop in the middle of the shale. Margo's hair shone behind the windshield, but Jack said nothing and made no sign. She backed up, opened the door, and the boys, catcalls emerging from the woods before them, climbed into the car. As Jack stood and watched, hating himself in his frozen silence, Margo turned toward the main road and, as if she hadn't seen him, picked up speed.

13.

"Why didn't you say something?" Marcello shouted, standing in front of him two days later. "That time in the store, then here on Monday. You're my father, after all. Why —?"

Jack put up his hands and shook his head, embarrassed. He wore jeans, a sweater, a pair of running shoes. Sitting in a car behind them and watching, Sonny, the pillar of strength and sobriety, thought Jack looked like an adolescent while Marcello, in green and gray uniform, dressed more like an adult than his father. Pulling down the visor on his cap, Jack leaned against the hood of Sonny's car and looked up at the trees.

"I'll tell the truth — I was afraid. I didn't know if you wanted me to be there."

Marcello narrowed his eyes, letting out a heavy, exasperated sigh. Jack cleared his throat.

"Are you kidding me, Dad?"

"Not a bit. Just ask him — Sonny."

Jack hooked a thumb over his shoulder. Marcello turned and looked past his father at a sallow, extremely dapper old man in a fedora who sat in the car smiling foolishly through the window. Jack shifted against the fender and, reaching out at last, stood up and took Marcello's hand.

"Look, I'm just not good with words, Marcello. I'm not like your mother — or Max. That's why I brought my friend here, Sonny."

"Words!"

The boy shook his hand free, and both Sonny and Jack saw that, before shoving it into his pocket, he balled it into a fist.

"Mom says you're just not ready yet. I guess she's right."

"Look, don't listen to everything she. . . ."

Marcello shook his head. "They don't want me to see you at all, you know. They don't think it'll do anyone any good — especially me."

"More like them, I'll bet."

Jack screwed up his face. Sonny turned away, clamping his lips in obvious embarrassment for intruding on their talk. Jack had invited him; dismayed at his own reluctance to speak to Marcello on Monday, he had telephoned Sonny that night to invite him down for moral support. Now, as the two let their eyes drift from the woods, to Marcello, and back to each other again, the boy smiled and, as if playing tag with one of his school mates, jogged his father's shoulder. "Hey, I don't listen to them *all* the time, you know. You were good to me. *Real* good, I remember, lots of times."

Jack shook his head. "When I was around, not embarrassing myself with drink, maybe." He glanced toward the giant oaks and pines, then turned away. Sonny caught his eye and nodded, trying silently to urge him forward. Finally, Jack draped his arm around Marcello's shoulders.

"It wasn't that bad, Dad. You could be a pain, but in lots of ways you were interesting. Even Mom says so."

"Interesting, but a pain? — Hey, I hope you didn't learn that from your mother!"

Jack embraced Marcello firmly, eyes tearing for the moment. It was hard not to feel awful for him, Sonny thought, especially remembering the story he had told of the last night he had seen the boy in New York.

"That fight with Max," Jack said. "Do you remember it?"

"Not much." The boy looked down at his feet, shrugging. "I don't want to. You were terrible. All three of you."

Jack slid his hands into his pockets and glanced into the woods.

"Mom thinks it was a difficult time for everyone. But she wasn't the greatest herself, I always tell her."

"She knows — My god, your mother knows what she's saying — more than I ever did."

Marcello stepped away. Head down, he muttered something that Jack could not understand.

"I couldn't hear you," he said.

"Wonder Woman!" Marcello said more loudly, throwing up his hands. "Max says that about her all the time. She acts as if she can fly."

Jack swallowed. For an instant, Sonny, watching closely, thought he saw him wince. "Your mother," Jack said. "Don't you. . . . Don't you and she get along?"

"Oh, we get along. It's just that. . . ," Marcello waved his hand. "You know."

"No, I don't."

"She's busy. School almost every day, and Max is at the office. I'm an only child, so I become a latchkey."

"Latchkey? —"

Marcello grinned. "That's what they call it. I'm alone a lot. Every Wednesday and Friday."

"Nobody's home — on those days?"

"Oh, someone's there: the gardener, or a maid, cooking for me. And sometimes him."

"Max? —"

"This is Bucks County, Dad. People hire cooks. Ours is named Elsie."

Jack said nothing. He looked at Sonny and shook his head. "When does your, ah. . . . When does Max get home?"

"Eight o'clock, nine, maybe later."

"Nine! — You mean you're —"

"Alone." Marcello smiled. "And awake. Just a latchkey loner on Wednesdays and Fridays. Often on other days, too."

Jack took his hands from his pockets and seemed to look at the sky for help. Sonny shrugged, wondering if the boy was laying it on a little thick. After a moment, all three smiled, Jack broadly, as if he had heard a cue. "Well," he said, "we have plenty of time to do something this Wednesday. Should we go for a ride? Sonny's skinny. There's plenty of room up front in the car. He knows your mother, too, pretty well."

"In that heap?" Marcello frowned, hardly acknowledging Sonny through the windshield. The car, Sonny's late life pride and joy, was a vintage Cadillac, huge, with fins and enough sleek chrome and horsepower to make it a highway weapon.

"It's all we have," Jack countered.

"Hey, I admire the waste," Sonny said, chuckling. "And can afford it. At my age, nobody's recycling me."

He grinned, and for the first time, Marcello looked him squarely in the eye, frowning. Jack blushed, but Sonny's smile took on brighter candlepower. Marcello nodded, firmly, and patted the shimmering fender.

"So, it's retro. Neat. Where does the young guy sit?"

"Here — beside me." Sonny extended his arm through the open door and took Marcello's hand, pulling him in. "I'm 'Uncle Sonny' to you. You can throw that knapsack in the back." Jack slid behind the wheel and, after embracing Marcello with emotion, dropped his hands to the wheel, and started the car.

14.

Both Jack and Sonny saw Margo in the way Marcello held himself erect when he talked, especially at the table in the hamburger place they visited that afternoon, and in the rightward tilt of his head, one ear forward, listening to, or answering, questions. He also had a certain kick to his back foot, Jack noticed one day a little later, when he hit a tennis ball. It could only come from Margo's genes, he said. The boy put his whole body into the stroke, driving the ball with every ounce of his energy, only to damn it when that stroke, energy, or a suddenly tricky wind, caused the ball to lose direction and fly long or wide.

As to evidence of himself and his own influence, Jack saw that Marcello was strong, that he had some real, though undeveloped, physical grace, and that, unfortunately, like his father, he could be very difficult to manage. Marcello *had* to fidget sometimes, and this physical need, this overwhelming itch, despite his mother's bookish intelligence, made the confinement of a full school day almost impossible to accept — as it had been for the restless Jack.

But more troubling was Marcello's apparent dissatisfaction — and loneliness — at home. He had few friends, did not see enough family: Margo, Max, and certainly, he added with emphasis, not enough of his father.

Jack nodded when he heard this. Sonny kept the silence from getting too deadly with half-remembered, half-made up tales of Anthony, Jack the little boy, and Carmine, meanwhile feeling a rush of sympathy for the whole Maresciallo family — and Margo. He expressed surprise that she had allowed Marcello to become so distant.

"Can't you talk to them?" Sonny asked, an infinite believer in communication. "Not even to your mother? She. . . ."

"Oh, I can talk to them."

"Well?

"They don't always answer."

Sonny looked at him, puzzled.

"No answer?" Jack said.

Marcello nodded. "Max" — he shook his head —"he's just like you, Dad. When he's sober, he's all right. But then —"

Sonny glanced at Jack, who folded his hands and looked down at the Formica table in the restaurant. Sonny said nothing, but he thought immediately of Jack's lonesomeness after Lillian died. "Does he talk to you — wrong? Or hit you?"

Marcello sighed. "He's not that kind of drunk, Uncle Sonny. He's like Dad. Sleepy, a little weird."

"Like your father?"

Marcello nodded. "He's not active. He just falls onto the couch." Sonny glanced at Jack, who looked embarrassed yet relieved. "And both of them are wrapped up in their work."

Jack looked at Marcello, the expression in his eyes a terrible mixture of despair and anger.

"Your mother's drinking, too?" Sonny asked.

Marcello shook his head. "Not a lot. She's got enough on her hands when Max is into it."

They stared at Marcello, each finding it hard to believe. But gradually, he gave them more details, and although some were exaggerated, Sonny and Jack conceded they found the story plausible. Max drank a bottle of wine with dinner, several scotches afterward and, over brandy or Campari, drifted off to sleep. When she came home, Margo read by herself until she got sleepy and took Max up to bed — as she had with Jack toward the end of their stay in Paris. "One bad drunk replacing another," Sonny said. "It's a bad deal for your mother — and you."

After that, Jack telephoned Margo, but she would not agree to meet or even talk. Finally, after several weeks of calling, he asked Sonny to drive down to New Hope again and speak to Margo himself. She had always talked with Sonny. And although they had not written much or spoken since her marriage, Margo had always liked him and might agree to a meeting. Besides, Sonny had always helped Jack since Lillian died. Margo knew that and might see it as an important favor for both of them. Franco agreed and with his encouragement, Sonny decided to try.

Marcello had recommended Tuesday as the best day to find Margo in the house alone: Max had *pro bono* business in court; she stayed in to write or prepare for her next day's classes. A little uncertain, Sonny sent her a note invoking their old bond and informing her that Jack had asked him to visit and speak to her about Marcello. He sent a second note two weeks later. Without an answer to either one of the notes, Sonny pressed the urgency of a meeting and wrote to say that he would arrive at her home to discuss Marcello the following Tuesday at three o'clock.

Still no answer came, but at least she had not refused his terms. On Tuesday morning, as a light rain splattered the windshield, Sonny rode down to Jack's and prepared to encounter Margo in the flesh again — after nearly twenty years.

15.

She didn't answer the doorbell right away, not surprising him, of course, but he persisted. While Jack parked the old Cadillac at the end of the driveway and waited, Sonny stood five, perhaps ten minutes, as close under the overhang as possible because of the late October rain. No lights shone in the windows, but he rang the bell and raised the knocker, rapping it sharply several times. Finally, after he had pounded five or six times and started down the steps in resignation, he heard a rustle behind him as the lock turned, saw the door open, and then, half-expecting thunder to explode or lightning to split the sky, looked up to see Margo face to face.

To Sonny at least, although it poured, everything else in the world remained absolutely silent.

"Margo."

He bowed, removing his hat and letting the raindrops fall directly on his head. "Hello. I've missed you."

She said nothing. Her eyes revealed distress and anger, but Sonny detected a sad resignation in them, too, as Margo looked beyond him to the car at the end of the driveway. Elegant, with her hair a simple swirl of flame on top, Margo wore black corduroys, a black sweater with a high and bulky neck, and smart black leather sandals. Sonny swallowed hard.

"I'm busy," Margo muttered, with no hint of politeness, much less a smile. Sonny faltered, in the position of a peddler momentarily or, worse, an intruder, the way many of his compatriots had been many years before. Trying to counter that, he marched up the steps boldly and, remembering his promise to Jack and Marcello, placed his cane firmly against the doorjamb. Before Margo could close the door, he pushed it wide and, without invitation, stepped into the hall.

"Everybody's busy, Margo, even a retired man like me. But today we should talk."

She stepped backward and turned. Without a word, she walked toward another door. Sonny found himself going through the next few seconds as if in a dream. Margo seemed to glide ahead of him; her sandals, though making loud scuffing sounds that he clearly heard, hardly seemed to touch the carpet. He closed the outside door behind him and followed Margo through an archway into the living room where she stopped in the middle of the room and, silent, still seeming suspended, waited. To his relief, she looked small here, especially among the formidable furnishings. The huge, gray room, formal — as only a 19th century interior's pretentious grandeur could be — stretched about thirty feet, with sixteen-foot ceilings and English windows opening to gardens on either end. A marble fireplace stood in one wall, a sofa and two chairs with carved walnut frames sat before it, a massive oak library table and built in bookcases reaching almost to the ceiling enclosed a reading area in one corner near the windows. A distant, old money look, Sonny thought. Within such magnificent surroundings, Margo had been working apparently. She glanced into the reading area near the oak table and then, impatiently, at her watch. Sonny tried to break through.

"I came here to talk, Margo. Please . . . give me a little time."

She walked to the table, opened a book, and, with a long, angry look at the rain on the window, sat and turned a page. "I have things on my mind," she announced, not yet greeting him, let alone saying his name.

She rubbed her forehead and ran a finger through the strand of hair around her ear. Sonny sat on the couch before the fireplace and, without success, attempted to catch his breath.

She wore jewelry, lots of it, an amount that, as Sonny later thought, she probably once thought tacky. Clearly, it was good and real: gold layered on her neck, gold circling her wrist, sparkling diamonds in her watch and ear rings. So much pure, cold cash — and to wear! He would have been ashamed to see Roseanna, Franco's beautiful wife, dressed that way. It diminished Margo, he thought, as if wealth had cheapened her.

She shifted her weight, tugging at the sleeve of her sweater and shaking free six more bracelets. So unlike the young woman he had met at Franco's wedding, Margo made him look at his feet and wonder about himself. He had left faint mud tracks, he saw, and again he felt like an intruder, more like her gardener than a visitor. Sonny stood immediately, turning to glance at the couch, ashamed to see the wet spots his trousers had made on the cushions. Excusing himself, he removed his shoes and, with a little half-grin, carried them into the hall, thinking, in anger more than sorrow, that he was worse than a gardener or peddler now — he was acting like a peasant. For one intense moment, Sonny thought of taking out his handkerchief and scrubbing the mud tracks. But when he returned to the living room, seeing Margo still at the desk, he said out loud, "To hell with it," and laughed. The faint spots had smeared by now and, to his eyes, looked hardly noticeable in the Oriental design. Taking a deep breath, he pushed all the nonsense about gardening and cleaning mud tracks away and strode across the room. Margo still said nothing. But as he approached her desk she closed the book and looked at him.

"We need to —"

She held up her hand and frowned. "I know Jack's been seeing him," she said, as if inspecting an inadequately trimmed garden hedge. "I've seen them out by the bus stop a couple of times. That's enough, isn't it? I don't even —"

"Margo, I didn't come to argue about the meetings. Jack didn't send me here for that."

Sonny nodded, attempting to smile with confidence. He waved and, as if at ease, stepped around the smudge marks on the carpet. Margo turned to look out the window.

"What does he want?" she asked.

"You know — He wants Marcello. To see him and spend more time. He needs his father."

Margo laughed, turning from the window but still not looking in Sonny's eyes.

"You've got to be joking, both of you. You walk in after years and say you and Jack want my son, as if he were a stored commodity I could trade."

"He's not happy here, Margo. Marcello says so himself."

"Get out! I don't want to listen!"

She spat the words, staring at the floor near his feet. Surprised, Sonny still didn't move.

But Margo trembled, terribly, as if shocked at her own display of emotion. Then the feeling must have passed, because with deep, quiet breaths and shoulders hunched, she leaned back and braided a pencil among her fingers. When she put it down, she looked at Sonny, square.

"Unhappy. Marcello told you that? Really?"

Sonny nodded, solemnly.

"I don't believe it. I don't believe my son would tell you that."

"Have you ever asked him yourself?" Sonny said.

Margo looked away, gloomily. Then with a short puff, she nodded her head, fiercely. "I don't need to. I know Marcello very well."

"He said it to us — not in those words, maybe, but he makes it obvious."

"Obvious. . . ." Margo glanced at her desk and again twiddled her pencil. Rain coated the windows beside her, and the outdoor light threw criss-cross patterns of running water across her face. She looked pale and, because of the gray shadows of the room, desperate. Still, Margo seemed controlled, and although Sonny wanted to state Jack's case as forcefully as he could, he knew that at this moment she wouldn't really listen. As if to prove it, she pushed herself from the table and cast a grim stare past him toward the door.

"For a ten year old, Marcello's had a lot of problems," she whispered. "Many of which we can't do much about."

"Margo . . ."

"His unreliable father, for instance. That's impossible."

Sonny held his tongue. It was the main point of her argument, of course. He knew it and had resolved, as an ambassador of good will, to try not to let her succeed. But the very sound of her voice broke that down. He shook his head, retreating. But looking into the opposite corner, near the window across from him, he saw a marble-top table with two or three brandy decanters surrounded by crystal glasses. Expensive decor for a movie set, he thought, but also for what Marcello had said about Max.

"Jack's changed a lot," Sonny said.

"So have I." She laughed. "Haven't we all?"

Sonny nodded — toward the table now. "Some of us have improved, Margo. Others haven't."

She hugged her arms, smiling — but shivering too, Sonny noticed. After a long look at the ceiling, Margo turned back to her book. Opening it, she began to turn a page.

"Margo. . . ." She said nothing, but he felt the doors close and the walls of her mind rise between them, as if she had walked into another room. He stepped to her worktable; with one sweep of his trembling hand, he pushed everything — notecards, pencils, pens, and books — onto the floor. Dramatic, he thought, and supremely stupid; yet even at that moment, Margo did not move or make a sound.

"You're not making it easy," Sonny said, nearly threatening her. "I've simply come to plead Jack's case . . . and mine."

Margo brought her hand to her lowered forehead and, silent, rested it there. She sobbed, her jeweled fingers threading through the strands of her hair. Sonny lost his composure then and, feeling sorry for her, as well as for Jack, Marcello, and himself, touched the back of Margo's head as if — he really couldn't say — as if to explain it. Margo slapped his hand away and swung around.

"Never, *never* touch me without my letting you! I'll call the police and have you thrown right out of here. I can do worse. Do you hear me?"

She pounded the table in anger, her fist clenched, shaking, and, despite his resolve, Sonny stepped back. Margo stared at the floor, whimpering, then glanced at his stocking feet, and with, tears running down her face, laughed as if he were a clown and she a bigger one for letting him upset her. She opened her book. With a voice that seemed to come from another corner of the room, she told Sonny that she did not want to talk to him or see him anymore. "Neither you nor Jack, and not even Franco," Margo said. "I'm doing my best, for my son and myself. That's just going to have to be good enough for everyone."

"Jack loves you," Sonny whispered. "He can help. He wants to help you and the boy."

She shook her head — slowly, exaggerating her movement.

"Margo, Jack's better now — a better man. Believe me. He's sober, for one thing."

She seemed interested for a moment but then, with a loud clash of bracelets, she hit the table again and began to pick up pads and pencils from the floor. Sonny stepped closer. Margo jerked herself away, warning him again to keep his distance. Then she bolted toward the other end of the room. "Not now, not ever again — I don't want you, or him, near me!"

"Margo —" Sonny felt his fingertips go cold.

"Forget it, I tell you! Tell Jack to see Marcello on the sly if he wants. You can both come to take him away for a few hours — every week, if you want. But stay away from me — out of *my* life. Both of you! It's too complicated already."

"I want —"

"*I want peace!* And I don't want you to ruin my life again!"

"Ruin it? Margo, I —"

"I do not want to look back — do you hear? I do *not*!"

She turned, pushed by him as she went to the hallway door and opened it. "Go, before one of us says or does something really stupid."

He hesitated. Margo rose to her toes, stared at the ceiling, and shouted, "Sonny! — *Leave my house!*"

"Can't I —"

"Not anymore — *Please!*"

"Margo —"

She was gone, up the stairs, door left open for him, clouds filling the sky in the gray world outside.

Sonny returned to the hall, put on his shoes and, without a word or glance in the direction Margo had taken, walked out of the house into the rain.

16.

"Strong, energetic, romantic in the bedroom, my men have been disasters in the rest of the world," Margo had written to Sonny once. Her father, a failed farmer, committed suicide by the time she was three; her first lover (when she was fourteen) grew up to join the Marines and, as she wrote, died miserably in Vietnam; a professor at the university (one she respected and worked with) abused her mentally and, sometimes, physically; and then Jack, the one she called the most loving and gentle of them all, just never developed, never went beyond high school sports, never found enough of himself, as she put it, to grapple with the world. He, she said, ruined their lives because he could not figure out who he was.

That was Margo's thinking, but it accounted for what both Franco and Jack had said to Sonny about her at the university. She had more sophistication than they did. At least it seemed that way because, to them, she knew far more than they about disappointment and pain. Now, as Marcello had told them, in Pennsylvania Max was sweet and loving to Margo only most of the time. He maintained good humor and energy most of his time at home, but occasionally work got to him. Within a couple of years after the move to New Hope, Margo had admitted to Marcello — although she didn't yet know there might be a cause — that Max drank too much scotch whiskey.

Clearly, indifference did not make her throw Sonny out of the house. But Jack had ideas of his own, and as they drove the turnpike in heavy rain that afternoon, he felt no desire to understand her thinking. Instead, he brooded, swinging between vengeance and forgiveness, planning some sort of legal action for days afterward, then deeming it not worth the effort. He missed his usual Wednesday meeting at the bus stop the following week, but then he heard from Marcello by phone and returned, again with Sonny.

Max and Margo had been arguing, Marcello told them. "A lot lately. They still don't want me to see you, but Mom says it can't be stopped."

"Max thinks it can?" Sonny asked.

Marcello nodded and looked at both of them. "I don't think he likes it that you came to the house, Uncle Sonny, especially inside. He said it never should have happened."

Jack clenched his fist, and although Sonny had never met Max, never seen him as a matter of fact, he admitted to himself that he felt insulted — and very competitive. "Let him worry," he muttered. "And let him clean those damn footprints on the rug."

In the back seat of the car, Marcello sighed. "Now he wants to pick me up at the school on Wednesdays, or any other day Mom can't meet me at the bus."

Jack groaned.

"Your mother agrees?"

Marcello shook his head.

"She didn't like the idea. She doesn't want any confrontations. But the other night, after they argued, she told Max to do as he liked. Just act carefully, she said, especially driving."

"Driving?"

Marcello put his thumb to his mouth and leaned back with his eyes wide. Jack nodded, straight-faced, while Sonny frowned. "She reminded him that Wednesdays were often busy for him too," Marcello said.

Sonny shrugged, angrily. Jack hung his head and looked out the window at the pavement.

Nudging him, Marcello said, "Don't worry, Dad. He didn't come today, did he? I think he just wants to be a pest."

Jack wrote Margo a letter —"neutral, friendly," as he described it. In it he asked Margo to let him meet Marcello regularly, according to some agreed plan, Wednesdays or any other day. He reminded her that Marcello wanted to see him too, and so, if all else failed, they hoped to continue their weekly pickups at the bus stop. It was unusual, but the meetings were convenient for everyone concerned, Jack said. Then he added, "Would you please tell Max to keep out of this? I don't intend to be a nuisance, and he shouldn't be either."

It was a fair letter, Sonny thought, and Franco did too. Yet, as had become her habit since the marriage, Margo did not respond, and the following Wednesday, when Jack waited at the bus stop, Marcello did not appear. Riding out to their house on his bicycle, he found the Continental parked in the circular drive and walked the bike through the woods to the backyard where he saw Marcello and Max raking leaves and pruning bushes. Max sang "Nessun Dorma" in a loud, half-humorous operatic voice as he smoked a cigar and raked. He drew into two high piles the leaves and twigs that Marcello stuffed into bags and carried to a shed beside the house. Clearly, they got along, though a little awkwardly, Jack would tell Sonny later. Max laughed a little too loud, attempting a friendly, fatherly tone, while Marcello worked silently, straight-faced, as if he were hauling leaves because he got paid.

During the next month and a half Max picked up Marcello irregularly, crimping plans for steady Wednesday meetings. Sonny advised Jack to hire a lawyer, but instead Jack wrote to Margo himself and telephoned a couple of times. He tried to be amicable, but although Margo had read the letters and listened on the phone, she did not answer. "I don't want to deal with it now," she told him and hung up the phone.

At the bus stop about two weeks later, as once again Jack watched Max turn into the shale road with Marcello in the seat beside him, his frustration pushed him to follow. Spotting the bicycle in the Continental's rearview mirror apparently, Max gunned the motor when Jack drew close, throwing stones and shale at him with his tires. Jack fell back, arriving at the house a few minutes after them, with a welt on his forehead.

Wiping blood and road dust from his face, Jack stood before the front door but, unlike Sonny, did not knock or ring the bell. When the maid, Elsie, round, short, and sixtyish, with rolled white braids at the back of her head, opened the door and politely asked him to leave the property, Jack rushed up the steps and, shouting, passed her into the hall. He found Max standing a few feet behind her, holding a fireplace poker in his hands.

Yes, it was November — cold — but a poker? Jack looked past Max into the living room and spotted Marcello standing between the couch and the fireplace, his arms full of logs, newspaper, and kindling.

"Dad," Marcello called, his eyes wide, seeming to plead with Jack for something, anything, an act to make things clearer.

"Get out of this house," Max warned, stepping between Jack and Marcello. "You — and your kind — don't belong here — ever."

Max let the head of the poker fall heavily into his palm.

"You don't have the right to keep my son from me," Jack told him. "Even in your own house. You can't!"

"I have all the rights, my friend. In this case, I have every one of them!"

Max raised the poker and stepped swiftly toward Jack. Marcello opened his mouth and, stumbling against the couch, cried out. Things happened more quickly after that, Jack would remember. He pushed past Elsie's flailing arms, stopped near Max just beyond the menacing poker's reach, and began to move as if to go around him.

"Basketball," he remembered thinking. "Let the scorer's instincts take over."

He feinted to the left, moved his head to the right and, not even blinking, stopped again. When the poker hit the floor beside his foot, Jack stepped on it, took Max's arm, wrenched it and, as the two tumbled toward the floor, he became a rebounder, giving Max a sharp, well-practiced elbow to the nose.

"The sound . . . I knew it," he told Sonny later. "Hollow, bony structure. Crushed. It was broken at the least."

Marcello dropped the logs and kindling, Max rolled and bellowed on the floor, his hands covering his bloody face. Elsie screamed and pummeled Jack's back as he rose to his feet and ran for the boy.

"Dad!" Marcello shouted. "What did you do?"

He turned from his father, shielding his eyes. Jack turned to see blood pouring onto Max's shirt. Wounded by Marcello's reaction, Jack lurched toward him, then spun and ran from the house, slamming the door behind him as he took the steps. On his bike, he pedaled out to the main road and headed toward his cottage. He swerved and almost fell twice, skidding on the pebbles. But he continued pedaling quickly, all the while expecting the crunch of tires from Max's Continental at his back.

FLIGHT

17.

Whatever buildings Jack noticed at Marcello's school looked old, well-cared for, and in place. People, as well as those buildings, appeared comfortable, graceful, completely at ease. Neither Margo nor he could have attained that sense of self-confidence, and it angered him at first that Max offered it to Marcello by inheritance.

"Welcome to the real world," Jack muttered to himself as he looked around. This place, this feeling was what Sonny and his father had talked about all these years.

"Feeling?" Sonny said when Jack told him. "What are you talking about?"

"It's there — *Medigahn*. . . ."

Jack grinned, looking almost shamed at the same time as he sat with Sonny in the Garibaldi lounge. His mouth tightened, and he described how he had found Marcello at the school almost immediately, walking between classes with some friends. Uniformed, talking soberly, they strolled on a tree-lined path between two brick buildings. Jack saw a couple of walkways leading off in different directions, toward a lily pond with a boathouse at one end, an ivy-covered auditorium at the other, and, beyond them, the main campus with a large athletic complex, soccer field, track, tennis courts, and gymnasium, all snuggled under the wing of a thickly wooded hill.

"But it was beyond that," he said to Sonny. "I mean the *medigahn* part. You couldn't make it or take it."

"Christ, Jack, what are you talking about? The after-life?"

"Comfort," Jack answered, shrugging at his own religious tone. "Unforced, honest-to-goodness comfort."

"Comfort. . . . That's all?"

"The first time I ever saw it. Or knew that I saw it."

Sonny laughed. "That's money, my friend. Very old money."

Jack nodded, glancing over Sonny's shoulder.

What else could he say? Sonny knew it, knew the magic of the feeling that had impressed Jack, but he still couldn't find it in himself to like it. Franco had driven them all down to see the school a few months before — as a possible place for his son, Francesco. It was all on the grounds, Sonny and Jack had seen: Longevity, the sense of things falling apart but presumed, despite that, to attract a certain kind of high-level clientele to help renovate. The Hammel house possessed it, Sonny knew. Some schools call it proud tradition, but Sonny's mother, prouder than most, would have refused to step inside the walls; and Jack's grandfather, Carmine, would have found them too fragile to stand near. "They'll fall on me," he used to say.

The morning Franco stopped the car in front of that ivy-covered auditorium on the main campus, Sonny, thinking of his mother and Carmine, refused, despite all Franco's coaxing, to leave the car. "This is a cemetery," he said, refusing to look up from the floor. "Do you want Francesco buried here? Why can't he go to school near us — something nicer, more modern?"

He looked out at the fallen leaves, the ivy, and the cracked, uneven slate walkways. He knew what lay here, but for the life of him he could not see why people like Jack and Franco envied it.

"Dad, come on! This is what you, Grandma, and I have worked our butts off for. We have to pass it on!"

"This is not what we have worked for! It is another people's life. *Idioto!* Not ours."

Franco squeezed the door handle and winced. He turned to Jack, who looked at Sonny. "Come on, Sonny. Take a look around. Please?"

"I will have nothing to do with it! My grandchildren deserve better, newer." Then, like Anthony Maresciallo, as Sonny regretfully said later, or like a stupid, stubborn child, he remained seated while the others left to enter the auditorium.

And like Franco, Jack still felt impressed that day — by the teachers and staff he saw strolling the grounds, by the trees and bushes perfectly placed, and especially by the little business-like students. Sitting and talking with Marcello beneath an oak, Jack observed them walking happily between classes. Carrying books in sacks and satchels, they occasionally ran after each other and teased, but more often he heard what he called "discussion" about Latin, trigonometry, business, and, especially, history.

Jack took Marcello's heavy backpack, and together they wandered out to the athletic complex. He studied the tennis courts, where Marcello introduced him to the tennis coach, a young, attractive woman with a bright face and graceful figure. The red clay courts, Jack saw, were kept in spotless condition. With the hill behind them, the fields stretching out to the east toward New Jersey, the ground and courts seemed like a setting for a French or English garden.

"A dream," Jack murmured to Sonny. "Margo achieved something for him — through Max. If he's unhappy, so are we all."

Sonny nodded, hearing how Jack had tried to convince Marcello of all that as they walked back to the rental car that morning. "This is a goal you've reached. Your mother has reached it — and not just for you, but for all of us. It's a place to spend the best hours of your life."

But Marcello, true to his Italian-American blood-type, at least as Sonny thought of it, told Jack that none of it mattered. He wanted his father near him, in New Hope or anyplace else. Max would not press charges over their silly fight; his mother wouldn't let it happen. They could still meet each other weekly, at school or somewhere in town. "I want to be with you, Dad," he said, his eyes pleading. "And I can probably get my friend's mother to lend us a car whenever you need to drive. We're good buddies."

Jack shook his head. "No secret meetings anymore. Besides, your mother and Max already know."

"Dad!"

"If I tried, they'd fight me and take you away. I don't want court battles, Marcello. I'm not good at that kind of thing."

"Then I'm coming with you, Dad. Now. Wherever you go."

"No, you're not —"

"Yes, I am! I don't like this place anymore. I'm sick of it — and Max — just because he went here!"

They stood near the car. With his mouth firm, Marcello approached it, opened the door, and slid into the passenger's seat. He tossed his green cap in the back. Bells on the school's central tower chimed to mark a quarter hour. Jack sighed as groups of students started out of classroom buildings, energy high, voices low and admirably controlled. Leaves shuffled to the ground, and as the two stared, a bus rumbled through the campus gate, its front tire noisily catching the curb of the sidewalk.

"You should go to class," Jack told him. "I'm leaving for a while. I'm not sure where, and so we can write. But I won't forget you."

"I want to go with you, Dad. Now."

"Marcello, I don't know where I'm going. Besides, I'll still visit. Your mother will let us see each other."

Marcello shook his head. Jack jiggled Marcello's backpack. Finally, he entered the car on the driver's side.

"It's been too long already. I want to go with you, Dad. I want to."

"You shouldn't," Jack mumbled, shaking his head and throwing the backpack over the seat. He jangled the keys in his hand.

Leaning across his father, Marcello smiled and blinked his eyes: thoughtful, dark green, certainly from his mother. He reached for the key ring and, glancing at the roadway, found the ignition key, inserted it, and started the engine.

18.

Three mornings later they showered and left his friend Bob Kaufman's West Side apartment to visit art museums. Early November, crisp and cold, with a strong wind blowing up from the south. It wasn't until they were at the Met, standing in the American room before Tiffany's glowing windows that Jack remembered a letter Bob had received in the mail the day before, slipping it into his racquet sleeve while they were hitting tennis balls inside a heated bubble. Now, retrieving their belongings at the vestiary, Jack took the letter out, saw it postmarked from New Hope, PA, and with Marcello looking on, put it into his jacket pocket.

"Mom?" Jack nodded. "That can't be a happy letter," Marcello said.

Jack nodded again as they headed toward the Met's main exit, dropping their metal buttons into the clear plastic container. "Worse," he said. "It's from Max. His law office, not from home."

"Mmmm. That's really bad, isn't it?"

"Let's get something to drink, okay? I want to consider this thing very carefully."

They walked down the steps, watching a bus go by them down the avenue.

"No matter what he says, Dad, I want to stay with you. Remember that. No matter what."

What do you do when a beautiful young son looks you in the eye, says he loves you and chooses your life on the run over an at home situation that has to improve his life? Do you send him away — force him to do the practical thing? Jack posed that question to himself as he looked at Marcello, his damp, cowlicked hair, and the dark green eyes. Love welled up so quickly in his heart that he couldn't speak, he told Sonny.

"I know," he muttered, barely breathing as the bus roared by.

Hand in hand, they walked to a coffee shop a block away from the museum, ordered cokes and stared at the envelope lying between them on the white glass-topped table. It was like a summons, Jack said. "I could send it back," he told Marcello. "This is a guess. They don't *know* that we're staying at Bob's. Your Mom's told them there's a possibility."

Marcello frowned. "They know, Dad. Mom does, or else it's a very good guess. Let's open it."

Reluctantly, Jack tore open the envelope and unfolded the letter inside. Silently reading, he found a surprise:

"Jack:

"*Do not show this to Marcello!*

"I am appealing to you as a fellow human being, and a father, not as a man whose home you forced yourself into and whose maid you attacked, not as a man whose wife is upset and frustrated because her son has been taken from her — abducted, most judges will say. No. I am writing to you as one man to another, one lover of Margo to another, asking you to have some simple human compassion.

"I am sick. My doctor has told me I will not live much longer than a year, and so each breath I take I regard as a treasure, each day a borrowed moment against the endless emptiness of my future time. Margo knows it. She has known it from the beginning and has consented to live with me so that the last few months or weeks of my life will find me home, reasonably happy, and (in the waning days of it) cared for.

"She loves me — I can't believe my good fortune!

"Marcello knows nothing about this, and we do not wish him to. We want him to be happy, optimistic. *I* want him to be confident about the future, as I am sure you do. But this step, Jack, this *misstep*, you have taken has called off every bet and plan. Margo is distraught and cannot sleep at night. I am frustrated and, yes, furious because what you have done shows that, even in a good, peaceful life, a man cannot control the safety and happiness of those in his household. I drink too much. More than too much. I am despondent often lately, which is natural, the doctors say. But I realize I have made life for Margo (and Marcello) very difficult. She doesn't deserve it; we don't deserve it. I might say that Marcello doesn't deserve what has happened either, but apparently (since Margo and I don't believe you would take him against his wishes) he has decided that he needs to be closer to you at this tender period of his life. Your friends at home tell us. . . . I won't continue. You know what your friends at home tell us.

"A proposal: Bring him back, preferably by Thanksgiving Day, and we will forget everything, the pain, the damage, and the legal ramifications. We will arrange for you to see Marcello regularly here in New Hope and, if possible, for longer periods during weekends or vacations wherever you are.

"You couldn't, rationally, wish for anything more. But first we must have peace, feel free of the burden of fear that your action forces on us, and that can only begin to happen when we see Marcello's face, here. Margo wants that more than anything else.

"*Please*. . . .

"Call or write. Bring Marcello home. You will find us flexible, even generous. But in case we do not hear from you, in case you decide to do something hurtful, I promise to pursue this issue legally, to find this boy for Margo (whom, you must know, I adore) until the very last breath of my being and — if possible — beyond.

Cordially,

Maxwell M. Hammel,

Attorney at Law"

Jack folded the letter and, with a heavy sigh, returned it to the envelope, letting them both lie on the table beneath his hand. Marcello stared at it and him, eyes sparkling as he sipped on his soda and made knots of the paper cover from the straw. "Not good, huh?" He wore a grim look on his face. "It couldn't be, Dad. Not from Max."

"It isn't bad. Just different." Jack tried to smile.

He shook his head and reached across the table to tousle Marcello's hair.

19.

Stable, reliable, as he had promised the Salvaggis he would be, Jack led Marcello to the car, drove over the George Washington Bridge, and turned south onto the New Jersey Turnpike instead of heading farther west. The gray November sky reflected dully in the water; above the trees, as they neared the Delaware, three or four pairs of hawks, soared and circled, like wind-blown mobiles, occasionally plunging toward earth as they spotted prey.

"I have to prove myself," he said to the pouting Marcello. "Maybe when you're older, in a few years, you'll choose to live with me. But at this moment —"

Marcello shook his head.

"I want to live with you, Dad, now! Not in a few years! What do you mean, 'prove yourself'! You've done that already — enough for me! What does Max know?"

Tears brimmed onto the boy's cheeks as he brought his hands down hard on the dashboard. Jack gripped his shoulder, looked away into the mirror, and saw his own tears as he fought to keep his eyes on the road.

Marcello blew his nose in a handkerchief. The closer they approached Pennsylvania, and Margo's, the more heavily he sobbed, and the more Jack felt he had blundered terribly. Since leaving the coffee shop near the Met, Marcello had sniffled and bawled constantly, sometimes shouting, even screaming at his father in the middle of a New York street, sometimes trying to reach him through a surprisingly adult use of reason and calm. But by the day they drove on the Turnpike and crossed the river into Bucks County, he had given up apparently, turning pale and suddenly looking ill. Jack stopped at a drive-in restaurant so they could use the restroom. Talking enthusiastically about other trips and future visits, he ordered sodas, held Marcello's shoulder as they drank them, and entered the car again to drive the last twenty to twenty-five difficult miles. He crawled, he told Sonny and Franco later, hardly pushing the speedometer over thirty or thirty-five, even on the highways. After one more stop, at Marcello's request, for a New Hope Burger King, they found the familiar black top road again, turned left at the barren, frost-covered cornfield, rumbled through hard woods and pine in low gear to the dirt path that Margo and Max lived on, and then practically inched their way, bumpy rock over frozen bumpy rock until they arrived at the circular drive near the large fieldstone Hammel house.

As they turned in Jack spotted Margo immediately — sitting behind a mullioned window with a yellow handkerchief in her hand. Before he could point to her, Marcello gasped, straightened to attention, and, without talking, peered out the passenger window and sobbed. The car slowed but still in motion, Marcello fumbled with the door's handle and lock, pushing it open. With a breathless shout, he leaped from the car before Jack stopped it fully and, from the end of the drive, ran toward the front entrance of the house, without so much as a word of remorse or a hint of regret to Jack.

"Mom, Mama!" he cried. "I'm home."

"Honey! I love you!"

She was on the porch, evidently sobbing herself, handkerchief rubbing at her bloodshot eyes. Jack parked, emerged from the car, and, galvanizing his courage, walked to the house.

He placed the red knapsack, two new tennis racquets, and a gym bag full of jeans and sweaters next to Margo on the porch. Nodding to her, he stood uneasily, watching the happy scene before him as Max, out of the house now, kissed and embraced the boy along with Margo. Max looked healthy, robust even, although there was something sad and waning about his eyes. But he and Margo, Jack had to admit, looked remarkably free of anger, just as Marcello, after all he'd said and threatened in the car, looked remarkably glad to see them.

"Thanks," Max said, his face buried in Margo's hair as Marcello and she embraced. "This makes everything fine. Happy."

"Do you want to come in?" Margo asked at last. She looked directly at Jack, mostly friendly through her tears, and pushed a strand of red hair back from her forehead.

Jack shook her hand, but the smile and remarkable offer of hospitality did not mask a certain strain in her voice.

"I have to leave right away," he explained, guessing her held down anger. "I'm visiting my father. Franco and Sonny say he's having problems, too."

"I'm sorry." Sobbing, not in sorrow so much as relief, Margo embraced Marcello again and looked down at her feet. He could see her bite her lips.

Jack said, "At some more comfortable time, Margo, I will give you an explanation for this. It won't be satisfactory. It just sort of happened, but it's not as bad as it must have seemed."

She inhaled deeply. "You don't need to," she said.

Jack raised his hand. "I know I've done stupid things before, but this time I thought I had to."

He hesitated, looking at Marcello, once again feeling his loving emotions well up in him. "We got to know each other better. For me, that makes all of it, *everything*, worthwhile."

"I hope so," Margo said. Her voice trembled as she smoothed back Marcello's hair.

"I know it was hard, but . . ."

"Dad . . ."

Jack turned to Marcello, clearing his throat and suddenly unable to speak. He bent to lift and hug him, surprised, he told Sonny later, that Marcello's arms, leaving his mother now, actually clutched for his neck and shoulders. Then more confused than surprised after he held the boy for a few moments, he put him down:

"Dad, don't go! Mom, don't let him! Please!"

Margo covered her face and glanced toward Max, who lowered his eyes and said nothing. Grim with the effort of checking his own frustration, Jack took Marcello's hand and firmly led him back to Margo's side.

"I have to go now, Marcello. I'll come down to see you regularly, I promise. — Should I just call when I'm ready, Margo?"

She nodded, clearly troubled as she held Marcello to her breast. "We'll work something out. Max will be in touch with you," she said.

"Here's an address up north — for the next month, anyway. I can't say where I'll be after that. Franco and Sonny will know."

Max took the piece of paper and, without looking, shoved it in his pocket. It was then — only then, Jack would later say — that he noticed the bandages. Covering a metal splint that spread out to his cheeks, tape crossed over Max's nose in the form of a large "X".

"I'm sorry," Jack said, waving vaguely toward the wounds.

Max nodded, silent.

"Write to me, Daddy. I'll write to you."

"Oh, Jesus, Marcello. . . ."

He looked at Margo and turned to the boy once more, lifting him skyward as he closed his eyes and embraced him. He would tell Sonny later that he felt like running. But at that moment, he glanced at Margo, put Marcello down next to her and, in the rush of emotion that followed, extended his arms. She shoved his hands aside and angrily pulled away.

"Not today. Not after all this."

He recognized the tone and expression — closed, determined — although she smiled almost apologetically. "This has been an awful, awful time," she muttered, after a pause.

Running down the steps, Jack blew a kiss, then went to the car and stopped, just as Marcello started after him. "The turkey!" Jack said. "We forgot!" He pulled a large platter from the back seat and raised it, awkwardly, above his head. It was covered with tinfoil.

"From Bob and Shirley Kaufman. Turkey leftovers. Do you want any, Margo? Marcello liked it a lot."

She looked into the house. Max, in his only direct reaction to anything Jack said that afternoon, lifted his newspaper above his shoulder and shook his head.

"Elsie has a whole tableful inside," he said. "It's our celebration — tonight."

Jack patted his stomach. "Hey, that's two Thanksgiving dinners, Marcello!"

He raised his hand, and Marcello, slowing halfway down the steps, laughed.

In the car, Jack placed the platter in the cooler and threw the car into gear. Trying for cheer as he left, he gave a hearty smile and a double beep of the horn as he let the car roll past the house. Marcello waved, struggling with his emotions and his mother's arms. Margo and Max stared, starkly. As Jack continued down the drive, finally reaching the road, the weight of the sad November afternoon descended on him. "I am not capable of taking care of him — or anyone like him," he said to himself.

He would repeat it later to Sonny and Franco. "Marcello needs more than just a father. He needs advantages — and a nourishing home environment — better from either of them, I think, than I can provide."

He passed the Burger King, accelerating, and sped along the black top into town.

OLD MEN IN LOVE

DED MEN IN LOVE

20.

Anthony Maresciallo said he had forgiven Jack everything: leaving the house, his wandering life with Margo, even the barely acknowledged grandson, Marcello. But now, with Jack in town again (living alone in a cabin a fifteen minute drive from the quarry), Anthony felt the old bitterness return. His own son, a Maresciallo male, taught tennis at the Garibaldi Club for that bastard builder and land-destroyer, Sonny Salvaggi; he had renewed acquaintance, at least distantly, with the savvy, money-grubbing *puttana* Margo; and capping it all he had visited Anthony in the hospital at Sunnyview to bring him a stomach-turning letter from the grandson, Marcello. Jack the Ripper. . . . No, worse than Jack the Ripper — a betrayer of every cherished rule he had been taught by his mother and father at home. In the name of what — Hating *Babbo*? Maybe. More likely basic human waywardness, the young people of these times.

> "*Dear Grandpop,*
> "*I have to send this to you in secret, because Mom and my foster dad, Max, don't want you to know where I am. They think you are bad for me, and they think my real father is bad for me too. Dad says you are nice, quite an old codger, he tells me, and some day I would like to visit. I also want to see Uncle Sonny again. Mom says maybe, but when I ask her, she won't say when. She thinks I have to age a little first — like parmagiano or pecorino, my dad says.*
> "*He also said you didn't feel well, that you fell in the mountains and hurt yourself. I'm supposed to say something to cheer you up — make you feel better. I'm not good at writing, but I hope this letter works. I hope you get better. I want to meet you — and hope it's very soon.*
> "*I don't know what else to say.*
> "*Dad says I should say I love you and close it. I do. I really do.*
> "*Yours truly,*
> "*Marcello M.*"

"*Puttana!* — Uncle Sonny," he mumbled.

Like Jack, Anthony lived alone now too, but he could never, ever see himself bringing his son, a traitor and still a *bambino* (over thirty years old, but incapable of the simplest responsibilities) back into the family house. My father's house. Elena's and Lillian's house. A house built with the

Maresciallo name and reputation attached to it, and where, in all probability, Anthony would die very soon. Alone.

"Last of the line," he said to Mary Ricardi on the day he left the hospital. She, along with Franco Salvaggi (a good, sincere doctor, though from a terrible, terrible father — and where's the justice in that?) had suggested letting Jack come home to share the house.

"As far as I'm concerned, my son is from another part of the world — another planet, maybe," Anthony said. "We will never get along. He will never be able to manage anything I leave. Not even share the responsibility."

And so, gradually, as Anthony healed from his fall (a small one, while out on some landscaping errands he had), he tried to settle into a modified routine of independence and solitude. Time to read, think, jot a few things down. Time to dot the *i*'s and cross the *t*'s of his lifelong education. He tried his best not to think of Jack or Marcello while he worked in his study or tended the needs of house and grounds, or even drove up the ridge to keep an eye on his interest in the quarry. He felt he owed that much to his father, Carmine, hard as the man had been on him and his wife, Lillian. And be-damned to the son who insulted his family name and relatives by living off a bastard's business, an untrustworthy bastard's business, instead of his own family's.

He spat at the thought of Margo and Sonny, still remembering them dancing at Franco's wedding, thinking of the stories he had heard about her own new marriage with the grand house in New Hope, and imagined what must have been her older husband's sickly gasps whenever he stood over the little *scamorza* for a piece of salty cheese. Yes, and despite all that the sad grandson, Marcello, not allowed to visit the people or place he descended from.

"Enough to make a man sick — and to think . . . of extremes," he muttered to Franco one afternoon, during a medical checkup. With all the despair that normally accompanied that kind of thought, Dr. Salvaggi had decided to send a visiting nurse and some other trained personnel to attend Anthony regularly until he healed. Through the fall and winter Sunnyview's aids, therapists, and nurses visited two or three days a week for a couple of hours each day. He paid, of course, and with his own money, not some indigent's public medical insurance. And despite his protests, their gentle hands, especially their pleasant dispositions, placed a better human perspective before his eyes. Eventually, his useless son visited and, confounding everyone — including himself, he admitted — Anthony let him come again.

They disagreed loudly, especially about Marcello, but actually enjoying the arguments, Anthony invited Jack yet a third time, mainly because he brought along one of Sunnyview's better-looking nurses, Rosalie Amato, whose quiet, confident disposition Anthony adored.

"Looking for company," Jack said to explain his father's actions. "The man's alone too much."

Under Rosalie's and the others' care, Anthony mended quickly and, by the following spring, drivers passing the Maresciallo house saw him in the front yard, walking normally, almost without a limp, although to some he had begun to look a little thin.

Franco didn't worry; lost weight would help Anthony move better, he said, and as the Salvaggi father and son drove into town the back way that March and April, Franco was pleased to see Anthony on the grounds daily. He had always loved gardening and was an early conservationist —"a tree hugger," Sonny called him after observing him one day in the woods near the quarry. He wore a straw hat and worked very hard, pulling weeds, hoeing, pushing a seeder and limer by hand to treat the soil. In the following, warmer months of late spring he began putting in bulbs, laying out food for birds, and pruning and watering trees. In the car Sonny felt jealous of Anthony's mobility, but tried to hide it. Though in his eighties, like Sonny, Anthony drove his pickup himself, hiked regularly into the hills above Maresciallo's Quarry, sometimes carrying a shotgun for hunting but, more often, taking field glasses to study wildlife on the family mountain — soon to become the *former* family mountain since he was selling the quarry.

"He knows the terrain," Jack told Sonny. "And has a good idea of what it's worth. He'll make sure he gets a good deal. I'll bet on it."

Sonny nodded, but inside he and others wondered. Practical as Anthony was, he was not in Papa Carmine's mold, having made some serious business mistakes through the years because he worried too much about the land. The big, really stupid move, everyone thought, was that a little more than five years ago, he had negotiated away the mining rights for the mountain to an out-of-state company, refusing the Salvaggi Corporation's competitive bid, as well as any other originating in the county. He thought they would build on the land rather than mine it. And immediately, the out-of-staters, while keeping the Maresciallo name on the quarry (as stipulated in the sale agreement), rolled in big machines, started strip mining, and then quickly bought their way into neighboring properties.

Town and county leaders launched lawsuits, citing economic factors, tourism, land-use precedents, and environmental guidelines. Several years of bickering and unproductive legal negotiations followed, and finally lawyers for both sides reached an out-of-court settlement where Anthony repaid much of the original sales price in return for a continued, practical interest in the mining. On the other hand, the mining company pledged to obey new land-use and environmental restrictions which, everyone knew, they should have obeyed in the first place since they were part of Pennsylvania law.

People in town witnessed gradual, minor improvements on the mountain for several months. But as they drove the roads around the quarry the following autumn, they saw and felt the alterations differently. The mountain, always a landmark, began to shrink before their eyes, and very quickly. Bare trees and brush disappeared or fell over by the day. The soft, blue-green slope of the horizon blurred into flat, grayish-brown chiseled spore. Giant shovels and dozers toppled trees and ate up brush. The Maresciallos had always done surface work by hand (having done it themselves, Sonny and Anthony could testify to that), but now large yellow and orange trucks and backhoes barreled over the mountainside, all followed by the muffled roar of blasting throughout the winter. In spring, conveyor belts and sieves carried away the mountain's slate and stone and sifted its granite to powder. The process, especially the rapid, seemingly unstoppable pace, ground away at Anthony even more than it did his neighbors and the members of the Garibaldi Club. He bore it for a time — defensively at first, and with a surprising touch of dignity — but then, during the summer, people began to see him change — in appearance and behavior.

He became secretive and quiet. Franco's staff psychologist talked of depression and loss of purpose — he even mentioned Alzheimer's disease — problems that, as eager dreamers, planners, and believers, most of the Italian-American patients at Sunnyview never really suffered. At the same time, the doctor worried that one day, in a fit of emotional despair, Anthony would drive his truck off a mountain road, or, worse, on one of his hiking excursions, plunge into a crevice.

But something different happened, a nice, positive event that people would gossip about for years as the lore and legend of Maresciallo's Mountain took force. Love, in the person of sweet, caring Mary Ricardi, entered Anthony's life, and people began to discuss its power as a kind of magical elixir. Anthony acted even more spritely and young, expressing genuine optimism after each visit with Mary. As everyone said with a smile at the

Garibaldi Club, Anthony appeared calm and glowing as only a grateful older lover can. Observing both of them, especially the happy looks on their faces, Franco and his staff encouraged Anthony to visit Mary often.

She responded appropriately, timid at first, yet memories from long-ago adolescence excited her increasingly. During her meetings with Anthony, she dared to take a step or two without the support of her aluminum walker. She started moving from chair back to chair back for support, and, eventually, with her long, tightly curled white hair bunching around her ears, she promenaded freely in the hall and outside in the garden, using only Anthony's arm or hand as occasional support. Mary wished to visit Anthony at his house, and, with Franco's approval, she was driven there regularly by Rosalie or Jack. On her returns, Franco noted her alertness and campaigned with the staff psychologist for regular weekend visits. The psychologist reluctantly agreed, and, going by Sunnyview guidelines, Franco convened a meeting of the entire medical staff to consider alternatives. With several gerontologists attending, they agreed to encourage her, as an experiment, to spend at least two weekends with Anthony during the summer.

"Who can stop them if they want to?" Sonny asked when Franco told him. "They're adults, with their own lives to lead."

As Franco drove him past Anthony's wrought iron gate on the first of two weekend afternoons, they spotted Mary and Anthony hand in hand among the garden plants and flowers. They walked slowly, their heads affectionately bent toward each other, and seemed to gaze intently at the surrounding landscape. Sonny's heart skipped with envy, but at the same time he felt moved to cry out to them with a co-conspirator's joy. The following weekend, while riding with his daughter-in-law Roseanna toward the Garibaldi Club in town, he saw them again, this time in Anthony's pickup as he drove up the ridge above the Maresciallo Quarry's grounds. Mary's flat, flowered straw hat and Anthony's chocolate brown fedora bounced in unison as they talked and pointed. Mary held binoculars while Anthony, steering with one hand, waved a cigar and gestured into the distance.

"*Cara mia!*" Sonny said aloud, barely containing himself as Roseanna smiled along with him. "Look how radiant they are! Is it really still as good as that?"

Roseanna blushed, hardly responding to Sonny's anxious look. "It's very lovely," is all she said, "truly very, very lovely."

On Monday, as Sonny followed an orderly pushing a wheelchair toward Mary's room at Sunnyview, he winked at the medical regulation requiring it and shook his finger. Mary Ricardi walked beside it, proudly holding Sonny's arm as she smiled at people in the hall. At her room, she sat on the bed, beamed at Franco and the staff psychologist awaiting her, and chortled happily when asked for an account of her weekend. Bouncing to her feet, she dismissed them both with a flick of her hand.

"I don't need a debriefing. I want to see my friends," she said. "I want to cheer them up, with this!"

Mary pirouetted, her eyes sparkling as she held her hands above her head. "I don't need a walker. I feel reborn!"

Franco and the psychologist nodded. They allowed Mary to stay at Anthony's several other weekends but remained cautious. Soon, staff and doctors heard talk of a wedding, and on his regular weekday visits, Anthony began to bring flowers and other gifts.

"It's sure," some of the patients whispered to the nurses. "We're going to have a ceremony."

"Dementia," one of the more envious said.

Franco ordered everyone, especially the paramedicals and staff, to keep their opinions to themselves. Rosalie Amato continued to visit Anthony frequently with Jack, and he, still in the cabin just the other side of the mountain, stopped by alone in the mornings on his way to work. Despite the rumors — and Anthony made no bones about it, especially with Mary — he could, or would, not be truly happy (or by extension marry), until Jack did something about his grandson. "I want to meet him," he told Franco, "finally — as any grandfather would."

Franco nodded and said he would do what he could to convince Margo and her husband to change their minds. He wrote several letters but, as usual, got no response. Some people believed Anthony had an old Italian man's obsession with his offspring and ought to give it up.

That fall townspeople saw his truck riding up the mountain roads near the quarry almost daily. Sometimes, they spotted Anthony walking in the woods or on trails alone, and they wondered what he looked for, especially with his rifle perpetually in his hands. Troubled by that image, Franco decided to telephone Margo himself. Not completely to his surprise, she was less than sympathetic to his pleas.

"I'm not happy with the thought of Marcello seeing him," Margo said.

"Or being anywhere near him, as a matter of fact."

"I know how you must feel, Margo, but Anthony's mellowed, as Jack has, especially with this new love. Why not let Marcello decide himself? He's almost eleven, he likes his father. Let him come up for a couple of days. He can stay with Jack — or us, if you prefer."

"Never with Jack. And I'm sorry to say, not even with you. Marcello's been taken away once already. We don't need that anymore."

"He brought Marcello back — on his own. You know Jack's changed, like his father. Besides, Rosie and I will take care of Marcello all the time, I promise you."

Margo said nothing.

"For a boy, especially a boy who's an only child, Margo, family is very, very important. The same goes for their grandparents. Kids are everyone's continuity."

Again, Margo did not reply.

"Are you there?" Franco said.

"Max is not well either," Margo said. "And I don't mean just physically. He suffered, really suffered, while Marcello stayed with Jack. He blamed himself, not Jack, for not being able to stop him. I don't want to see that happen again. He's a genuinely caring man."

"Suffering? — Is it an illness, or do you mean the extended drinking? Because if you do, Margo, I can't . . . Margo?"

Franco bit his lip and held his breath in the silence. Not even a hum or dial tone marked his mistaken question.

21.

November passed, December too, and no note or phone call came from Margo. Jack and Sonny wrote friendly, pleading letters, but she replied through her husband in business-like, legal terms. For more than a year, Jack continued his weekly meetings with Marcello at the bus stop and received nothing but evasive formal memos from Max concerning commitments.

A second February passed, yet another summer and fall, and then, almost three years after their escape to New York, in the beginning of that winter, with a light snow already falling, Franco received a letter from Margo about a possible visit. The message was short but to the point. She would travel north with Marcello early in the new year and, to combine business with pleasure, conduct a little research for a personal project, a report on some subject in the field of gerontology, an intense interest of hers, one she had been studying and writing about for a class at Temple.

She would spend a week, maybe two, in the Poconos. Marcello could visit his father and grandfather, but she herself particularly looked forward to seeing Franco's work at Sunnyview. She had heard a lot about it from her professor, she told him. On another note, she especially looked forward to seeing Sonny Salvaggi who, she wrote, had sent her a tender, sympathetic letter about Max and Marcello a year or two ago.

"Tell your dad," Margo said in the letter, "he still owes me a waltz that we never completed at your wedding."

Franco Salvaggi smiled when he read that sentence, and when he repeated it to his father later with a humorous glance, Sonny let out a quiet, prolonged sigh. The lights from the ceiling sparkled on his balding skull, and Franco, happy about the letter, patted Sonny's shoulder good-naturedly. "She hardly even mentions Jack or me," he said. "How do you do it, Old Man?"

Frowning despite himself, Sonny waved his hand.

They sat in Sunnyview's solarium. Mostly beige and blue, it now had seasonal touches of red and green, pleasant Christmas things, with rustic chairs and couches that Franco's wife, Roseanna, had chosen for their hominess. As Franco directed, a Vivaldi flute concerto piped from speakers in the ceiling, with patients playing backgammon or chess and several reading or working at laptops while swaying absently to the music.

"Where do you think she'll stay?" Sonny asked as he leaned back. "Here, at the motel in town, or with one of us?"

He squirmed a little, making the rungs of his chair creak as the leaves of an elephant-ear philodendron tickled his neck. Franco shrugged, folded the letter, and slid it into his pocket.

"She could stay anywhere, Dad. I doubt seriously it will be with us."

"She's certainly welcome at several places," Sonny said. "Maybe at Jack's even, but probably the motel. She can certainly afford it."

Franco nodded, but then shook his head and shrugged. Jack's cabin was certainly large enough, but Franco's house was different — spacious, elegant, good for any number of visitors. She'd be fine there, he was sure.

As everyone agreed lately, Franco Salvaggi had grown to look very much like his father: slim but soft at the waist, lanky in legs and arms, with a handsome dignity to his face and slightly receding hairline (much less receded than Jack's, he liked to think), and always a welcoming greeting. He favored bulky corduroys, sweaters, and athletic walking shoes over his father's lifelong dapper attire.

"Invite her to our house!" Sonny said abruptly. "Invite her for me! Better yet, call her right away."

Franco nodded, then looked away. He rose, poured a cup of tea from the urn on the table next to the wall and, after adding sugar, returned to the sofa. He hadn't seen Margo in almost ten years, but he remembered her vividly and appreciated her intelligence. He especially remembered her with Sonny on the evening of his wedding, and the image of them dancing together before all those guests still made him blush with embarrassment . . . and pleasure. His father hadn't forgotten, he knew, and Margo apparently hadn't either. As Franco recently told his wife, Roseanna, some sudden spark must have ignited between them and probably still burned, but the conscientious, filial side of Franco wanted to ignore the details. His father had lived and certainly sinned, Franco knew, but it was not for him — even in light of his mother's lonesome, desperate death — to see his father as anything but sober and upstanding: occasionally romantic to a fault, but never unrealistic or drooling.

"I have to ask Roseanna's permission first, Dad," Franco said. "And Jack's got to agree, too. Margo's bringing Marcello up to visit him and Anthony, after all. Not the Salvaggi clan."

"Anthony Maresciallo!" Sonny waved in disgust.

"That's what the letter says. Marcello is eager to meet his grandfather."

"Huh. . . . Grandfather." Sonny looked at Franco and shook his head. "Anthony's hardly talking to Margo at this point, my boy! As to Jack, it's a given he'll do anything she says. It's his nature."

Franco looked at Sonny and nodded. "Still . . ."

"*Basta!*" Sonny looked furiously around the room. Several patients stared at him and grinned at his sudden loud voice. He apologized and continued. "Anthony Maresciallo has to give in a little to the rest of the world, my boy. Especially with Margo."

Franco nodded immediately. Taking it as silent agreement, Sonny let out a large sigh of cigar smoke from his mouth. A huge grin lit his face, although he remained silent. Anthony owed him something. He had proudly given Jack a job teaching tennis, managing geriatric fitness programs, and generally making sure things ran smoothly around the Garibaldi Club. Jack had performed very well so far, surprising everyone, including Sonny, taking time off only on Wednesday afternoons to visit Marcello in New Hope. Anthony had to appreciate that and not try to dominate Margo's time.

But the whole discussion was eventually made useless. Within weeks of Margo's letter to Franco, Max sent another memo from his office canceling everything they had planned: no more appearances by Jack or Sonny at the Hammel house; occasional visits with Marcello, but only if Margo specifically put it in writing when he and Jack would meet; and worst of all, Marcello would by no stretch of the imagination spend important vacation time with his father and grandfather — whether Margo travelled with him or not.

Shaking in disbelief after reading the memo, Jack called Max's office twice, only to find him unwilling to talk. On Franco's advice, he telephoned Margo again, but she told him she didn't have time for "quibbling." "Simply put," she said, "I don't feel comfortable with you and your father seeing him. I don't like the possibilities."

"Margo, I thought this would be different. In fact, I thought you agreed with me that it would be good for him to spend time with me and my father. Things are not the same here. They're more peaceful."

Margo let out her breath. "I just don't have the strength to do everything you want, Jack." After a long pause, she added, "I have several other responsibilities."

He held back a long moment himself. "Margo, that's Max talking to me, not you. It doesn't sound like you at all."

She said nothing.

"'Responsibilities.' I can smell a lawyer's strategy all the way from here."

Without another word, she hung up on him.

Jack pressed the redial button right away, but Margo didn't pick up the phone when it rang. He tried to calm himself, and after speaking to Franco and Sonny that evening, he agreed to meet the Sunnyview company lawyer to explore legal options. The lawyer did not give much hope after hearing about Jack's past behavior, but he suggested that they approach the Hammels with all the procedural weapons available. Jack wouldn't win a case in all likelihood, but within a year or so, they would probably wear out and accept an out of court settlement that he could — or would have to — live with.

"Live with?" Jack said, shaking his head. "I'm Marcello's father."

The lawyer shook his head. "It's tough," he answered. "But it may be better than what you have now."

Jack stood up and started for the office door. "I'd rather do things informally," he said. "This is my son and former wife. It may seem stupid, but we still have family ties."

The lawyer stared at him. "Max Hammel," he said. "Don't overlook that man. He's a lot more than family."

But Jack continued his weekly drives to New Hope anyway. Marcello gave him news, and occasionally, very occasionally, he heard something from Margo. Her tone was distant when they talked, yet from time to time, she seemed to regard him as a supportive friend. In the long run, Jack reasoned, it would go better for him and Marcello if he worked, as Sonny had always advised, to continue to build her trust. At her request, he drove down and took the boy to tennis classes or piano lessons whenever she was busy. Margo seemed grateful and increasingly asked for help. Jack felt sure, he told Sonny, he would get what he wanted from her — faster but more quietly than a lawyer. More important, it would be in his own low-keyed, *husbandly* way.

22.

Max died slowly, quietly, not of drink but of a gradually expanding tumor, which was his real problem, Franco told Sonny. "Stage four. It's an illness Marcello just didn't understand."

In the middle of that winter, Jack drove to New Hope more frequently to help Margo and Marcello as Max declined. Snow covered the mountains as early as November, and by December heavily carpeted the woods surrounding town. By February Jack could no longer count on driving to New Hope at a moment's notice because it snowed practically every other day. Skiers from New York and Jersey loved it, filling town stores and crowding restaurants, turning sidewalks loud with noisy bickering that only businessmen and townhouse developers enjoyed. Jack continued to work hard at the Garibaldi Club. Sonny saw that he developed activities for skiers' children and senior citizens, as well as provide tennis lessons for anyone who asked. He found doubles partners for matches, filled in as a player himself when tourists wanted an after-noon off the slopes, and occasionally played one or two younger players who made him sweat a little when they played a match. Traffic on the roads near the Salvaggi property increased, growing heavier but more silent, too, because packed snow muffled engines and tires no matter how fast they moved.

A skidding car ran over a neighborhood dog. In the beginning of March houses down the hill lost roadside mailboxes to a swerving SUV. Roseanna worried about Beatie and little Franco trudging to school or crossing into the snow-filled woods along the opposite side. Sonny, re-membering Margo's loss, her son's puzzlement, and Anthony and Mary's new-found love, felt the world, too large, too complicated, and certainly too much with him. One early morning at the end of winter, as he slept in his cottage in back of Franco's house, Sonny heard a muf-fled thump and loud metallic boom in the distance. It echoed through the woods and quite literally shook the walls around him. He thought it was a car running into a tree or a drift, but something alive near the woods outside roared for nearly half an hour afterward. It filled the morning darkness with a horrible, plaintive cry that went directly to Sonny's throat. Eventually, he saw the lights go on in the main house and followed when he saw Franco, searchlight and shovel in hand, walk out to take a look.

They saw a huge black bear on its stomach at the side of the road. A thick, dark liquid flowed from its mouth and surprisingly small ears. In the searchlight's beam Sonny saw tire tracks through the new-fallen snow lead up to the largest of the spots, curve sharply to its right, re-verse, and then, blurring as if from haste, continue forward. Struggling, but critically injured, the bear pawed at the snow on the berm, leaving large, blood-red scratches as it heaved for breath and support from its legs and feet. It lurched weakly once or twice, howling and snapping its teeth whenever Franco or Sonny stepped near. Franco phoned the police, and in half an hour they saw a van rumble up the hill, a cruiser of two state troopers trailing it.

By then a couple of early morning motorists had stopped to look. With Franco, Sonny, and the police, they stood mute as the bear panted, gurgling blood and bile while it scrambled to rise. Suddenly, one of the troopers shrugged. After a word to his partner, he went to the cruiser, pulled out a phone to talk to headquarters, then returned with a rifle and, still not stepping within reach of the animal's claws, shot the bear three times before they hauled it away in the van.

After a few moments of conversation with the bystanders, Sonny and Franco walked back to the house and tried to eat breakfast.

Two mid-week storms blew through shortly afterward, but eventually, toward the end of March, the weather started to turn warm — at least for a week. By the beginning of April, Margo called to say — the doctors were certain this time — that she had called in the hospice nurses for Max. They would administer pain-killing medicine but no food or liquids unless he asked. She asked that Jack come down to New Hope to stay with Marcello while she sat with Max in a bedside vigil. Sonny immediately agreed to let Jack go for as long as he needed, and Franco called Margo to offer his own assistance. He tried to reassure Margo about last minute medical procedures, and she, of course, dreading the inevitable next few steps, could hardly respond to him. Although still holding a grudge from their last meeting at her house, Sonny wrote a friendly note of condolence and support.

Jack left for New Hope during the second week of April, by chance the day before Max Hammel died. He attended the funeral with Marcello at his side and, after the burial, while they talked alone in her room that night, Margo grew feint and collapsed in Jack's arms. "Nervous exhaustion," the doctor said after Jack called him.

Max's grown children and their families stayed at the Hammel house a few days longer, but they finally agreed to leave Margo and Marcello alone until she could make concrete future plans. They were amicable, Jack said, but a little uneasy because, despite a signed pre-nuptial agreement that kept his and Margo's assets separate, Max had informed his oldest daughter a few weeks earlier that he was about to adjust his will. No one knew for certain whether the changes had been made, and certainly no one knew what they were.

"*Madonna,*" Sonny said. "This smells like trouble!"

Franco — and others at the Garibaldi Club — nodded, a bit gleeful, as if they had known it all along. And when Jack returned from New Hope with details of the specific changes, people could not help smiling or winking about it. According to the most recent documents, Jack told them, Margo would receive trusteeship of the Hammel property (ownership would pass ultimately to blood-related heirs) along with a hefty, hefty chunk of Max's money — for her and Marcello.

"Marcello, too!" Sonny chortled. "She did it! He's taken care of."

Jack nodded.

"The poor Appalachian farm girl," Sonny said, shaking his head. "There were heavy medical bills, I'm sure, but he must have carried more than enough insurance."

"The best," Jack answered. "As far as I can tell, she won't owe a thing." Sonny shook his head and shrugged. He felt happy for Margo, but inside something grated.

"She'll be comfortable," is all he could say. "She's done very well."

Jack said nothing, and after a moment he nodded. "But in fact, there's more than money in this mess, Sonny. Margo wants to do good with it, not just take a ride on a classy yacht. In fact, she's talking about a medical foundation — something for cancer and age — to name after Max. She'll talk to Franco about it when she's here."

Sonny pursed his lips, wishing he could smoke a cigar, which was against Sunnyview's new rules. "A foundation? — We'll see what that does for his memory, my friend. You never know — especially now. . . ."

Jack raised his hand, shaking his head, and grimly placed his finger on his lips. "I know; I know what people are going to say, Sonny. But I don't want to hear any of it — especially from you. When Margo's here, you'll see things differently, I'm sure."

Sonny clenched his lips and remained silent, but he tried to remember his comment at Margo's house about people getting better with time. She, herself, was certainly making an effort, it was clear.

They walked through the long hallway between the Garibaldi Club and Sunnyview, settling finally in the broad solarium to wait for Franco who was finishing afternoon rounds. Patients and one or two of the staff members might walk in and hear them now, but on seeing the bright room empty, they continued talking. It was then Jack brought up another issue.

"Margo's already funded a couple of independent projects near Philly," Jack whispered, stopping as one of the aids pushed an empty wheelchair across the room and into the hallway. "Those are for kids."

"Good for her," Sonny said. "I'm sure she knows what she's doing."

Jack nodded, grimly. "She's talking to professors at Penn, developing themes for research projects on medicine and health at both ends of life, especially — and this will interest Franco — gerontology. She wants to start a foundation in Max's family name."

"Gerontology! — In the Hammel name!"

Jack nodded.

Sonny stared out the window toward a large expanse of sunny lawn and tried not to let his emotions — bitter and confused now — leave his throat as he held up fingers and thumbs, rubbing them together before his eyes. Jack would defend Margo on his own deathbed, Anthony had always said, even with her knife sticking from his chest, and even as she refused him a helpful drop of her cool, now rapidly bluing, blood. Still, and Anthony would have to admit it, too, Margo was attempting to do good. And she did have something special. She touched people when she looked at them, brought out emotions that anyone could feel.

"It's nice helping others," Sonny said with a frown. "But it's a pity her generosity won't serve you — a man who really loves her and has for a long time."

Jack blushed and looked away toward the door.

"It's true, and everybody knows it."

Jack turned and looked into Sonny's eyes. "Well, it serves us all," he answered. "Franco, me, you — and thousands of others. That's what foundations do. Margo will be here in a few weeks, as soon as the estate clears up. She'll talk to Franco about medical developments that he can take advantage of for everybody here."

Sonny nodded. He lifted a cigar from his shirt pocket to his mouth and — keeping within the letter of Franco's new-fangled rules — chomped on it as if it were a piece of candy. "At one point, I could only think of Margo in glossy, frilly things: yellow, red, gold," he said. "That was my mistake, but whoever expected to see her in widow's black — with unselfish intentions?"

"It's changed her, Sonny, even since you talked to her. You'll be surprised at how much has gone on."

Sonny smiled.

"It's more than money," Jack said, shifting in his chair. "I'm sure of it. This is character too, so don't make fun of her."

Sonny grinned again, but as Jack spread his hands on his knees, gripping them and leaning forward, as if against a strong headwind, something crossed his mind and made him look outside.

"She's certainly impressive," Sonny admitted.

"I'm telling you," Jack answered.

"Possessions can do that." Sucking on the juice, Sonny bit his cigar more tightly. "Margo's powerful, very powerful right now. Don't forget that."

Jack shook his head. He stood on his feet and crossed the solarium terrazzo toward the window. After a few steps, he hesitated and looked at Sonny. "Power's *your* word," he said. "Just like my father. But when I went down to see Margo, she was needy, weak, the very opposite of powerful. Now she has a look of purpose. . . . And real physical joy — because she's doing something good."

Sonny blinked and answered almost angrily. "What the hell are you talking about? — She's free and in control, no geezer like me can drag her down."

Jack looked out the window. It was clear he had listened to Sonny's words. "Margo's look surprised me," he said. "But then I understood. I remembered it well, and now I'd know it anywhere. You would, too."

"Look? Wait a minute, Jack! What are you —?"

Jack grinned. Sonny flushed at that, the expression on his face suddenly flustered by the clear meaning in Jack's dark eyes.

"Are you saying —?"

Jack nodded. "It tells me where her real life interests lie."

"Life interests! . . . Are you —? . . . You're absolutely crazy, you know that? "

Sonny stared at Jack and, with a dead weight now sitting on his chest, surprised himself by feeling very jealous. He threw the chewed cigar to the floor and, angry, stomped on it.

"It's yours, I hope — isn't it? Otherwise, this is a land grab! You — or she. . . ."

"It's Max's," Jack said. "I'm sure of it."

He uttered the words evenly, serious, but then he caught Sonny's eye and turned pale.

Sonny raised his fist, pumping it above his head, almost in triumph.

"She gave Max his continuity," Jack whispered, "with her body — and just in time."

23.

No one at the club — or anyplace else in town — believed Jack, of course, but out of respect neither Sonny, Anthony, nor anyone else said anything. Whenever people talked, Sonny just shook his head, crossed his fingers for good luck, and inwardly pounded his chest in pride and vanity over Jack's earnestness. What was in it for the him, people wondered, and at the Garibaldi Club they asked about Anthony and Marcello. Hadn't Anthony, snob though he was, gone through enough over his grandson and their separation? Why should Jack father another child for that woman, only to let it be claimed by a dead man and his will?

Anthony heard about it and must have thought the same thing, especially before, as everyone knew, Margo and Marcello approached his house a few weeks later for a meeting. Margo wore widow's black and, Anthony noted, held Marcello's hand with a compelling sense of duty and care. She also carried a bloom of color on her cheeks that had nothing to do with makeup. Franco saw it, Roseanna and other women responded to it when they spotted her walking among the lawns at Sunnyview: self-assured, solid, at last comfortable with her station and her age, she seemed to glow with more than health. At Anthony's, Jack walked modestly behind them, presenting her first to Mary Ricardi at the entrance to the house, and then to his father in the living room. Finally, Jack took Marcello's hand himself and stood expectantly before Anthony who, biting his lower lip, rocked forward and backward as he sat in his broad wingback chair.

"Pop, this is for you, at last: Marcello. Marcello, meet your grandfather."

Marcello extended his hand and mumbled something. "*Bon giorno, Nonno*," Anthony thought he heard. Jack said that on seeing Anthony tremble, searching for words, he himself felt like falling to his knees and begging forgiveness.

"He's heard a lot about you, Pop — a lot of it good."

"I'll bet," Anthony growled, but smiling.

He shook his head. Swallowing and extending his hands, he let his fingers run along Marcello's arm until they reached his face. "*Bon giorno*, my dear, dear boy." He let out a breath, took Marcello's dark-haired head, and pulled him closer, kissing him lightly on the cheek. "I'm not nearly as bad as your father will tell you," he whispered. "Your mother and father have no idea what it means to an old, old man with no one else around — especially grandchildren."

He hugged Marcello, sitting him on his right knee and leaning back to study him. Both Jack and Margo saw the same thing in that particular moment: a three-generation resemblance in nose, chin, and eyes.

"A fine, fine face," Anthony said. "With a wonderful head of hair, and a few stringy stogies standing up in back. — Isn't he wonderful, Mary?"

"Marvelous!" Mary said. She smiled.

Like Margo's, Mary's cheeks glowed at that moment. Seated across from Marcello on the heavily antimacassared sofa, she rose to her feet, shifting from leg to leg for a moment to loosen her muscles, then walked closer and touched Marcello's shoulder while he hung his head.

"The boy writes, Mary: wonderful, expressive letters to his grand-father. He'll do more, I'll bet — maybe become one of those great Italian writers. Remember this visit, Marcello. You'll want to write about it someday."

"Two letters, Grandpop. That's all. I'm no author." Marcello smiled, raising a pair of fingers like a victory sign.

He squirmed when Anthony embraced him, turning to Jack and Margo in embarrassment. But at a nod from Jack, Marcello threw his arms around Anthony's neck and kissed him. Anthony gasped at the gesture, returning it with enthusiasm and smoothing back the hair on Marcello's forehead before letting him go.

"You may not be an author yet, but your words worked, I assure you. You put them down, and — you can ask Mary Ricardi, if you don't believe me — they did this old dog some good. Real good."

"Moderately," Mary said, smiling. "But in your grandfather's case every little bit helps!"

Anthony gently slapped her shoulder. "Hey, what are you talking about, Mary?" He coughed, then coughed again, an overwhelming spasm of contentment that he smothered with a blue bandana. "Those letters sweetened my disposition," he said, squeezing the bandana back into his pocket.

Mary grinned. "If I didn't know you already, Anthony. . . ."

She braced herself on his shoulder, rose and walked into the kitchen. When she returned, slowly pushing a teacart with a tray of pastries on it, she sat on the sofa next to Margo and poured coffee and tea. They talked quietly for a while. Mary and Jack said little, mostly listening to Anthony discuss the house, the property, his father, Carmine, and his mother, Carmella. He opened an old family photo album, showed Marcello pictures of a few somber paintings by Carmella and Jack's own mother, Lillian, went on about the fine walnut furniture and handmade lamps his father had imported from the Mezzogiorno, and pointed, through the windows, to the mountain and quarry that Anthony called, with regret on his face, the "former" family business.

"We must drive up there sometime," he said to Marcello. "It was the foundation of this house — and this county. And it might have been yours — was yours, in fact — but for. . . ."

"Pop, don't go into that. We don't need it."

Jack held up his hand, his knees rattling the cup and saucer he balanced in his lap.

Anthony closed his eyes and breathed heavily, as if to gather himself. "Your father disinherited you, my boy. Not me. Remember that if you ever wonder about your history in this family."

Jack steadied the cup and saucer with his hand and looked toward Margo and then his father. "Let him start out with a clean slate. Please? Marcello isn't a part of this stuff."

Anthony raised his voice. "He has no choice. Family name or not, the earth from that mountain is in this house, and in his blood!"

"Well, in fact he has a choice. And I do too. He won't be a part of all this garbage from another time. I've made mistakes, lots, but I've also made a new beginning. Let him start with me."

Margo stared, surprised, she would later admit to Sonny, at how firmly Jack stood up against his father. She drummed her fingers on the arm of the sofa and, looking from Jack to Anthony, glared at both of them. After a moment, Jack shrugged and, white-faced with frustration, gazed at his feet. Mary turned to Anthony, who looked surprisingly uncomfortable, too, and shook her finger. "Jack makes sense, I think. Let's try to be pleasant. This occasion won't allow for viciousness."

She poured a second cup of tea for Marcello and passed around the plate of pastries. Seated, she expressed regret to Margo over Max and asked about her plans. Mary had spent a few years in Bucks County, she told Margo, and always thought fondly of that part of the state. "Will you stay in New Hope?" she wondered.

Margo nodded, a little uncertainly. "Marcello and I are attending nearby schools. So, more than likely we will. . . ."

"And," Anthony interrupted, "will you live in your . . . your husband's house?"

Saying nothing, Margo lowered her eyes.

"Pop —"

"Is it in fact yours now?" Anthony said. "I mean the house?"

He leaned forward. Anthony knew nothing about the will or the prenuptial agreement, as far as Jack knew, and he had heard only rumors of her pregnancy. Yet a broad grin broke out on his face as he looked at her, and he pounded his fist on the arm of his chair. "It is, isn't it? I can see it on your face. As I — as everyone, except my innocent son here — would have expected!"

Margo placed her cup and saucer on the table. Her back erect, she glanced angrily at Jack and heaved a long sigh. "My husband left it in my care. That's all. Legally, it belongs to his last surviving heir — or most recent."

"Recent —?" Anthony looked at Marcello, forgetting himself and what he knew. A visible lump grew in his throat as he turned to Jack and then to Margo.

"My grandson?" he said, studying her face. "Marcello? Did he adopt —?"

Margo shook her head. Jack raised his arms and started to rise from his chair to explain, but with his father and Margo on either side, he could not bring words to his lips much less stand. Instead, Marcello broke the silence. "There may be something else happening," the boy said. "Mom's going to have a baby again, my sister, she says, by Max — and she's over forty. It's like a miracle. Some of my friends think it's weird, but I'm happy to have a larger family."

Marcello smiled, obviously happy.

"Max's —?" Mary said, startled.

Anthony stopped her, raising his hand and glancing around the room. He counted backward — aloud — the number of months and weeks since he had heard that Max was sick.

Mary picked up the coffee pot and poured again. "Anthony, these things just aren't right for a young boy to hear — no matter how smart he is. And it's none of our business. Let's discuss more appropriate things."

"He brought it up, Mary. His mother must have told him something." Anthony grinned.

Mary said nothing. Her hands shook as she reached over the teacart to fill Anthony's cup with coffee. He added a shot of Canadian whisky. "We're just getting to know Marcello and his mother," she said. "There are other things for a grandfather to talk about with his family."

Anthony nodded, reluctantly, but Margo smiled. She told Jack and Sonny later that it had not occurred to her, until that particular meeting, how things might look to other people. "There will be some DNA testing," she said.

Sonny doubted her, of course, but then again Margo couldn't be expected to know how much people at the club would agree with him, or how much Jack had revealed to friends. With just a glimmer of understanding now, Margo said she felt uneasy, and a little later that day, when Mary took Marcello outside for a tour of the Maresciallo grounds, Margo asked Jack to go out with them. She said she wanted to talk to Anthony alone.

24.

"Tell me," Anthony said, when the others had left, "will Marcello get anything out of this?"

He pointed across the coffee table and, absentmindedly almost, tapped his forefinger on the pastry platter.

"He'll be taken care of — by me, of course. Jack may want to help some too, but I'll be primary."

"Jack. . . . The Garibaldi Club tennis pro." Anthony sighed and shook his head, lifting the last of the pastry from the platter and chewing it.

"My only son. In case you didn't know, Sonny gave him the job to get my goat."

Margo looked through the glass doors to the clear blue sky, dropping her gaze and centering on Jack in the garden. With his arm around Marcello, he followed Mary Ricardi and talked as she pointed to some freshly turned soil and sprouting buds.

"It's good, honest work. More important, it's something he enjoys doing. If you would —"

Anthony shook his head, genuinely sorrowful, it seemed, and interrupted her. "Let me talk to you as I would a man, a businessman. Why not? — You know more about money and finance than my son does. Innocent — he still doesn't understand the world, I think — except for painted pictures, maybe, and tennis balls." He smiled, nastily, Margo thought. "I understand clothes and school, and other immediate needs, will be paid for. But, honestly, is there anything else? — Any — what do you call it?"

Margo shook her head.

"Inheritance — financial inheritance — for Marcello? I'm told your husband was very rich."

Margo blushed. "Later," she said, coolly resisting the impulse to tell Anthony to mind his business. "But it will be from me. My husband left us plenty of insurance."

Anthony closed his eyes. He started to moan, building the volume slowly, as if he were mourning at a wake. After a moment, he opened his eyes, looked deeply into Margo's, and, licking a pastry crumb from the corner of his mouth, hammered the table with his fist.

"'We'll take care of him,' he swore to me!'Margo and I will do what's right!'"

"He'll be comfortable, Mister —"

"With what? A lackey's salary and the leavings of a shyster lawyer — or his widow? Does your old friend, that skinny, elegant *sfatcheem* over the hill, Salvaggi, pay Jack enough to support himself, much less a family? Does he want to?"

"Mr. Maresciallo, he'll —"

Anthony raised his voice over hers, shouting each syllable: "Mahr... ESS...shee...ah...LO! You speak the language, Jack says. Say it right."

He laughed, and, as if to spite her as Margo turned to look through the doors again, rose heavily from his chair. Daunted at first, then steeling herself, Margo stepped around the coffee table and squeezed in front of him. She stared directly into his eyes, her face not more than two inches from his jaw.

"I have come here, Mr. Maresciallo, at Jack's request and, he tells me, your begging. I don't intend to take any more of these cheap shots — about my dead husband, me, or anyone else. We are taking care of Marcello — better than you did Jack, from what I've heard. And if you can't be pleasant now, I won't stay in this town. You will not see Marcello again, ever. I guarantee it."

Anthony sputtered. She raised her voice again and stopped him. "On the other hand, if you are friendly, or at least civilized — a very unusual behavior, from what I'm seeing — I could arrange to have him stay here a few days, perhaps a week — if Mary is here and Jack stays with him."

"Stay! Here? If —"

Margo shook her head and pressed her finger against Anthony's chest. He looked, and felt, absolutely solid to her — perfectly healthy and robust, she told Franco and Sonny. With Max's pitiful dying image still in her head, she began to doubt all of Jack's and Franco's special pleading on Anthony's behalf. This was not a weak, sickly man.

"Remember," she said. "You have nothing, absolutely nothing, that I want, including this house. I am not a gold digger."

Anthony grinned, but it was weak and false, she could see. He was preparing to take her on. On his terms.

"I want nothing from you," Margo repeated, slowly. "This house, which I believe you have always thought others covet, is filled with awful memories. I wouldn't want my son to live here, and I'd be surprised if Jack wanted to."

"My —"

She leaned closer, shaking her head again.

Anthony bellowed. Raising his large hands and clenching them, he seemed about to bring them down on Margo's head when Jack, who had listened outside the door after seeing them through the window, burst in with a cry and rushed across the room. He took Anthony's wrists and pushed him backward, onto a chair. He took Margo's arms (she had a tight grip on Anthony's shirt front by then) and coaxed her down to the sofa next to the chair. As Anthony started to rise again,

Jack put his finger to his lips. They heard Mary, followed by Marcello, talking and laughing as they entered the kitchen from the garden.

Anthony frowned but remained quiet. As Mary and Marcello entered the living room, the five of them smiled at one another and, for a moment, looked happily at the budded spring branch Marcello held out before them.

25.

Margo had planned to stay until the end of that month, but because Marcello said he liked seeing his grandfather and Sonny a lot she decided to remain a little longer. On educational leave from school, the boy studied subjects on his own, aided by his mother, Jack, Anthony, and Mary, while Margo worked from time to time with Franco to gather information and, as she called them, "models and concepts" for her foundation that would honor Max. She visited Sunnyview daily, observing the staff, interviewing patients, talking to families, and, with their permission, studying patient medical charts. She talked about a donation, or investment in Sunnyview, something to help Franco with his work — also, she said, as a memorial to Max.

Sonny met Margo occasionally, inviting her to lunch in the Sunnyview cafeteria, seeing her once in a while at the Garibaldi Club, talking to her privately in town at some coffee shop or restaurant. But never, Sonny regretted, did she visit him or Franco at their house. She looked very much the same, like her younger self with some twenty years of added experience: trim figure, now fitted in dark skirts and slacks instead of jeans; flaming hair, but with mature, lighter gray highlights here and there; and the sharp, inquiring eyes that, to Sonny, seemed to look beyond and, sometimes, through, a man. She carried herself very quietly now, less playful in her talk but obviously much more confident. "A loss," he sighed to himself when he remembered her freshness at Franco's wedding, "but a proper one."

"Experience," she told him, during one of their few private conversations. "And, yes, I admit, years. Time chips away at your self-confidence, don't you think?"

Sonny shrugged. "Time. . . . I've seen so much of it that's all I seem to know. But if you can't keep your confidence, what woman can?"

Margo lowered her eyes. A portion of Sonny still felt special in her presence, even after their difficult last meeting. He knew that memory, filled by her close body, caused that good feeling, and it was as if time had not progressed between them. He felt the emotion physically, all along his backbone and at the tips of his toes, generating a more youthful bounce in his step the moment he saw her, whether in Franco's office, a store downtown, or in the gardens at Sunnyview. Surprised by his own natural excitement, he felt competitive about it too because he had not yet come to terms with the last meeting at her home.

"Women have a harder time with self-confidence than men do," Margo said, "especially as we age."

"Age. . . ." Sonny waved at her. "There's only one thing you can do."

He drew a finger across his throat. Margo looked at him and laughed.

Sonny nodded, laughing a little too, partially at her and the subject, mostly at himself. They were in the laurel garden at Sunnyview and, because of that, "Confidence" was the last word he would have used to talk about himself. "You have a lot going for you, my dear young lady, especially your age. In addition, you now have something substantial to go with it. Most of the people here live in a different world."

She looked at him quizzically.

Sonny grinned. "They're on Medicare or some other kind of public insurance. You have possessions, power, and a lot of life still ahead of you. Those are the kind of things men feel confident over."

Margo winced, then, he saw, she began to flush with anger. She rose forcefully, and Sonny let his fingers slip from his cane as he sought her hand. For a brief moment Margo let him take it and, looking into her eyes for a long, long few seconds, he could think of nothing better to do than pat her stomach and then the bench.

"You have that in your future too," he said. "I envy that second child more than anything. I always wanted to have a larger family."

Grudgingly, Margo settled next to him, even snuggled a little closer. In one of the more open spaces in Sunnyview's gardens, they sat in silence and watched the afternoon sun shimmer through the trees from across the lawn while a breeze from the west carried the scent of fresh grass and budding flowers that floated him back through many years.

Above them laurel bushes drooped; maples and oaks had begun to take on their annual pastel haze. It occurred to Sonny more than once during this talk that he had met, and consequently always thought of, Margo in springtime colors and, after more than twenty years of envying Jack and the other men she must have known, here she sat next to him again, warmer air still surrounding her. A man, he thought, might do silly, even stupid, things.

"At least you won't have to struggle," he said. "You'll have the wherewithal —"

"Wherewithal," she interrupted, shaking her head. "Money — that's what everyone thinks." She patted her stomach and laughed, almost bitter. "This is not going to be easy at my age. Or inexpensive."

"Yet it will add something; something wonderful for you and Marcello — and uplifting."

"Uplifting?" She smiled, almost as if he were her son. "Sonny, I never thought I'd hear such an idealistic word from you."

He shrugged. "Family is all. Nothing else really matters where I come from."

She looked at him, doubtful. "You believe that, don't you?"

He nodded. "I've made awful mistakes, but what other choice do people have?"

"For some people. . . ." She nodded, but added nothing more.

Sonny pointed to his head and touched his heart. "I've learned some things," he said, "not as soon as I should have — or as my mother wanted me to. When I was young I thought ecstatic moments with women, traveling, sleeping with them, would last forever. But my old body tells me another story today. Kids. . . . Grandchildren. They make my life . . . worth living right now."

Margo shook her head. "Maybe. But I have things I want to do yet, and I'm not that young."

Sonny looked at her, puzzled.

"Marry," he whispered quietly, without thinking. "Marry someone who loves you, with no reservations."

Again she shook her head.

"Marry me," he said at last, after taking a deep breath.

Maintaining a firm grip on the cane he now plunged deeply into the stones at their feet, Sonny stared earnestly into her dark green eyes and grinned, feeling himself turn pale. Nothing had been farther from his mind as he started to talk, so now he tried to act as if he were making silly jokes. He smiled, trying for a contented look, but after a long pause

Margo shook her head again, grimly.

Or, he wondered, was it tenderness?

"Sonny, dear. . . . You're trying so hard, but I can't help thinking you mean it." Her eyes swelled over, breaking his reserve even more as she collapsed against him. "It's sweet," she said. "You've always been — even in the difficult moments — very, very sweet."

"If you could marry Max, you could marry me. For a few years at least, I —"

Margo snuggled closer, reached across his arms, as well as her own swelling stomach, and touched his moist cheek, driving away all Sonny's pretense and distance. The light had begun to change. They sat in the shadow of a pair of lilac bushes whose green branches had not yet begun to flower. Sonny could dimly make out the windows of Franco's office in the building behind them. At first, because he thought they might be seen and laughed at, he pulled himself away from Margo, whose head now lay quietly on his shoulder.

"I can give you the same things he gave you, I assure you. I can buy — or build — a new house. I can afford to send Marcello, and this second child, to a very good private school. I can leave them more money than they have now — more than he left, because there wouldn't be a pre-nuptial agreement. And, I assure you, Franco and his family need nothing. The companionship —"

"Sonny — good lord. . . ."

"I mean this, Margo! With all my heart!"

He tapped his breast.

"But it's not what I want — or need!" she whispered.

Margo swallowed, leaning back and looking into the sky, as if to compose herself. "You are sweet, and precious, Sonny. With all the madness and rough karma about you, I've always had to admire that special, genteel quality in your soul."

She wears black now, Sonny thought. She will always wear it, probably, because she is widowed early and will not let herself forget. Black blazer over black dress and heels, he noted, and a small black pillbox hat with a dark veil pulled over her eyes. Still the hair around her ears burned like an off-colored flame, heating his heart enough to boil it away. For twenty years he had thought of her, and for twenty years, whenever he hated or felt jealous of anyone, one image of her had remained: a young girl in a cheap gold dress whom he had danced with at his son's wedding while blossoms fell around them like a gentle spring-time snow. Now, like that early snow, she had melted into an entirely different form.

"I have never given you credit," Sonny said, "for all that you did." Margo looked at him. "I mean for me, opening me up, bringing me back from. . . . Franco's mother died — terribly."

She frowned, although with kindness, then nodded. "You made me feel loved, Sonny. For two important nights and a good many years. I needed them. I could be young and careless, I thought. I wish we could have stayed that way."

"You have — for me." He thumped his chest, creating a heavy, hollow sound against the bones. "And I am not saying that out of obligation!"

She sighed, lifting her head from his shoulder and looking at the sky. A warm breeze shivered the lilac and laurel behind them, provoking a quiet, stirring hush. Drained, Sonny turned to Margo, allowing himself to feel the warmth and comfort of her fingers on his arm.

"Well," she said, wiping her eyes and smiling sadly, "it certainly hasn't been a pretty time, has it? We might have blown something important. To think some loud music, a few hours under the same trees, and —"

"And nothing!"

". . . nothing," she said, smiling at his bitter voice. "And more than nothing for these many, many years."

Sonny sat back, tears rolling freely down his cheeks, and laughed out loud despite himself. He lighted a cigar, blowing out puffs of smoke that rose and spread quickly in the wind. The smoke must be visible through these trees, he thought. Franco and others might see them, certainly Jack.

"Did it mean anything permanent?" he asked. "I mean back then?"

She nodded, smiling. "I moved fast, but nothing much emotional got by me in those days. I felt it."

"Felt it?"

She nodded.

"Then why did you, or didn't you —?"

"I didn't want to be pinned down, Sonny. You were too solid. Jack — his physical energy, his career: Simple as that, I thought he had talent. I still do."

"Talent? Is that all you thought about, really? And your careers?"

"At that time I was determined to grow up, make something of the world — and myself. I didn't want another father. Especially one like you!"

She grinned, with a bitter anger Sonny could feel at the center of his heart. "So I got a son instead. Two of them, it turns out. Maybe a third is on the way."

Margo began to weep, quietly at first. Tears poured down her face as she and Sonny joined hands firmly, amicably, and, at last, separating, folded them in their laps. When Sonny turned to speak, he saw an innocent schoolgirl beside him, praying.

"Max — you really loved him?"

"Mmm, very much." Margo lowered her eyes, sobbing. "He was kind, the good, kind father I always feared — and wanted."

Sonny said nothing. He closed his mouth while he leaned back and stared into the sky. His eyes burned, and he took a long, long draw on his cigar. *To hell with the smoke!* He thought. And its visibility! He exhaled heavily into the wind.

"I know what you're thinking, Sonny. But don't torture yourself. With Max it was extra special. I can't explain."

He looked at her, thoughtful. "He bought you things?"

Margo nodded, reluctantly. "Flowers, paintings, books. But insignificant things too, like certain kinds of cookies. He never seemed to tire of making me happy. Or trying to."

"Even with the drinking —?" Sonny swallowed. Once again, she lowered her eyes.

"The man was lucky. The man was simply. . . ." But Sonny stopped himself, seeing a new path of tears sliding down her cheek. He leaned across the bench, caressed her stomach, slightly swelled, and felt Margo's arm, then her shoulders, and then her warm, electric fingertips against the insulation of his old man's wrinkled flesh — for the first time in what seemed like two dozen lifetimes.

"Sonny, Sonny! I still miss him! I do!"

"Margo, I. . . ."

They did not kiss; Sonny did not touch any part of her face with his own. He simply rested his chin and lips against her hat and then her hair, patting her back as they embraced and he thought absolutely nothing except, at that moment in the growing dark, that the sun still shone, the sky held purple azure for a few moments, and the breeze, beyond the grass and leaves, carried a precious fragrance he could not name.

"Margo, I'm sorry, so very sorry for all the pain you've had!"

He pulled out his handkerchief, held her away from him and, lifting the veil on her hat, patted her eyes and cheeks. She took the handkerchief and blew her nose, giggling now. Leaning back, he let his hands rest on his thighs as he clenched and unclenched his fists. They sat in silence and watched the sun gradually disappear. Margo removed her hat and shook her hair. Replacing the handkerchief in his jacket pocket, she nodded and looked toward the sky, her expression still intense.

"You chose to have it, Jack said."

"Max wanted it," Margo said. "No, he demanded it. Really."

"Of course, I can understand. A man who's. . . ."

She nodded once more. "He wanted to show how much he loved and trusted me. I think he was sorry . . . that we had to part so soon."

She sobbed louder. Opening her purse, Margo pulled out a wad of tissues and wiped her eyes and nose. Sonny turned away, sickened.

"So he argued, really yelled at me now, as if he *were* my father — Marcello never understood this — and told me that I had to do it. For us. For what we meant."

"Max told you this?"

Margo nodded. "To prove that there is hope. And purpose, too. He said it would keep him alive — longer. At least long enough to see the child."

"It wasn't Jack? It was — It was really —?"

"Of course it was. One of the last times before his — Oh, shit! It's so pathetic!"

Tears layered Margo's cheeks and lips.

Weightless, yet somehow held down by everything, Sonny took her in his arms, handing her his handkerchief as he brought her close. He felt ugly, miserable; his only comfort was that she felt awful and maybe his presence helped. Again the wind rustled the lilac behind them. Sonny felt Margo's hair against his chin, and, in reflex despite all his self-disgust, he felt himself groping, turning his mouth and head to seek her lips. He trembled, trying not to think of age or the way he looked. She gave him her neck and cheek. He kissed them both, hungrily. Then he let her go, sat back, lighted another cigar, and, breathing deeply, stared at his shoes, his hands folded firmly in his lap.

"It's mine," she said. "Mine and his."

"Not Jack's — truly?"

She shook her head. "I tell you, Sonny. I'm carrying it like a mission, a holy one."

She smiled. Sonny put his hand on hers — it was resting on her abdomen — and felt something, something furtive.

"Sonny, do you think people. . . . Your friends. . . . Our. . . ?"

"Shhh! It doesn't matter," he said. He put his finger to her lips and cried, moaning. "No matter what happens, what anyone says about you, or it, or us. I love you; I will always love you. I have loved you all my life!"

MARESCIALLO'S MOUNTAIN

26.

Feet grow longer, widen, and, at a certain age, their owners (in this case Marcello) grow clumsy. Soon he lacked grace on the tennis court (and, probably, the dance floor), but on visits to his great grandfather's town, Sonny saw, despite physical changes, the boy improved in many ways.

Smart, sure of himself, he no longer pestered his mother for things he wanted. He spoke politely, requesting permission to phone or visit, paid attention to Margo willingly and, when he stayed with Jack or Anthony, concentrated completely on schoolwork, complaining less about chores he was asked to do.

The boy had matured, Sonny told everyone, earlier than his father had, perhaps because he now had a younger sister, Tina. What's more, Marcello had grown more manly in appearance, showing signs of his father's and grandfather's thick arms, wide shoulders, and chunky, muscular legs.

Marcello's long nose protruded over boyish, determined lips, and as he reached thirteen his adolescent eye harbored a look, one Sonny noticed almost by chance one day, that was very much a Maresciallo's. As Jack and he played tennis or took long, fast-paced hikes together, Marcello spoke to Jack of his hope for a different, more generous life. "People are too selfish," he said, "even you and Mom — and Sonny — though you don't mean to be."

"Your mother's always been thoughtful about others," Jack said.

They would be paused on a trail above the Water Gap, looking down on the river toward New Jersey. Hills rose across the way, and to the left, if they looked carefully through the trees, they could see Maresciallo's Mountain, what had once been the family quarry.

"Mom always needs to produce," Marcello said, "make things happen. That's good, but I think there's more to life than that, don't you?"

"More than producing things?"

Marcello nodded. "Because you use things up, too. I want to give value to my time, without having to show something material for it."

Jack nodded, taking a quiet, lengthy, breath. He knew Marcello saw things differently than he had, suffered at the loss of trees, the crushed animals, the retreat of nature as more and more people left New York and New Jersey to come live near them in Pennsylvania. Marcello wanted to improve the world, and so far his only effective response was self-imposed vegetarianism. A gentle sentiment, Jack thought, at odds with the world he grew into and the activities and appetites his broad, thick-limbed body nurtured. The boy had heard such ideas at his private school, Sonny thought, but Jack sensed that Marcello felt them personally and had committed to them on his own — a little like his grandfather, Anthony. "He thinks human beings need to earn and exercise a general love," Jack told Sonny, "because the world needs extra care."

It was a late fall day, a few years after Max died. As they stood in the forest above the river and followed a connecting path to the Appalachian Trail, Jack found himself admiring his son, especially the expression of commitment on his face as they hiked. Looking across the valley, he observed the bare, scarred rock face, the sheered tree trunks torn out and tossed aside, the evidence of men and machines under a corporation's control. The quarry had essentially decapitated a mountain — Maresciallo's Mountain. Despite himself, Jack thought of his father and recalled his own struggles with Anthony, struggles somehow embodied in his father's wish that he take over the family business, but that he continue it the way Carmine had — by hand.

"You mean you want to add value to time," he said aloud to Marcello. "I thought art would do that for me — at least the sculptures I was doing. But I'm ashamed to say nothing good ever seemed to come out of it. Maybe because I produced insignificant things. And my father — he just worked to preserve his father's mountain, until all he did was preserve its name."

He cast his eyes downward, spotting a maple log on the side of the trail. Automatically, he thought of what he would have done with it once — maybe a nice wood-carved human figure, maybe an abstract shape with hunks of limestone and shale to play on textures. But value? Who knew about that? Maybe it was just a way to keep his hands busy, pacify his anxious mind.

He shook his head and looked at Marcello. At this stage of his life, Jack thought, he needed to concentrate on things — fundamental things — his son's future, a winter hearth that wanted warmth, a woman he still loved in need of attention. Looking up at what had been the family mountain, he thought of his father and grandfather again, of what they had done to secure his boyhood comfort. He needed to do the same for Marcello. In the distance, someone squeezed a trigger and an engine began to whine. It sputtered and coughed at first, caught and began to roar. Soon another tree would likely fall. His friend Sonny was building houses again.

"This is the best —" Jack whispered, reaching out for Marcello's arm. "You are the best, most valuable thing — today or any other time — that I have ever done."

27.

"You cannot allow the boy to forget us. You cannot allow his father and mother to alter our memory."

Us. Our. — That was Carmine, Sonny thought, probably referring to Jack, or maybe to Sonny himself. No one, certainly not Jack or Margo, knew. But apparently Anthony, in his last letter to anyone, had decided to make the memory of his mother and father, or at least their family name and history, indelible: *Maresciallo's Mountain.* People had no idea how it happened, why, or where and how, at more than eighty-five years, Anthony had developed the energy and strength, especially after becoming rather sickly of late.

Investigators do know that within a month of Marcello's arrival that last year, the first of the millennium, and shortly before Margo came up for a visit too, in the middle of an early spring storm that dwarfed anything the town had experienced during the past winter, Anthony drove off with his grandson, "escaping," as Margo angrily told the police, leaving in his pickup truck whatever warmth and sanity Jack's cut firewood and Mary Ricardi's friendly presence had contributed to him that winter.

Nor does anyone — even Jack and Margo — know exactly what Marcello's motives were, whether he felt upset with his mother (or father), whether Anthony had somehow, perversely, struck a companion cord in his idealistic earth saving heart; or whether the romance of the mountain and the tales his grandfather told about Carmine during the afternoons they spent together had somehow lifted him out of caring for the world he knew through split-up parents, a baby sister, and school; or whether it was just the inner hell-raiser that Jack had witnessed upon first seeing him in the art supplies store in New Hope and then again on the day they left his private school for a Thanksgiving adventure.

"Fairness," is all Marcello would tell Jack afterward. "I wanted to be fair to Grandpa Anthony when everyone else, except Mary, doubted him — including you."

Whatever it was, Marcello left with Anthony willingly, the night before a party Franco and Sonny had planned at the Garibaldi Club for him,
his sister, and Margo. Sneaking out the bedroom window of his mother's
rented cottage near Sunnyview, the boy left just as the early spring
snowflakes, huge, wet, already sticking to the grass as well as parts of the
road, began to pick up force and speed from the incoming wind.

He carried a blue knapsack, boots, a couple books, warm socks and
an extra pair of jeans instead of his usual tennis clothes, sneaked from
the garden behind the cottage, then down a tree-lined road past Jack's
cabin (where a night light still burned) and then on down the path at
the end of the woods, where his grandfather's pickup, lights out, waited,
engine smoking and at idle.

"*Ciao, Nonno.*"

"*Ciao, figlio mio.*"

Marcello opened the door, climbed in, and the truck, with just its
parking lights on, lurched forward, Anthony patting Marcello on the
shoulder with one hand and carefully directing the vehicle along back
roads toward the opposite end of town with the other. It wasn't until
they reached the main highway that Anthony switched on the headlights
and they began to talk.

"You have everything you need?" Anthony asked. "Warm clothes?
Boots? They're calling for snow tonight."

"Everything, Nonno. And my Dante."

Anthony smiled, his pale unshaven face and bright white hair gleam-
ing in the light of a passing car.

"New hat, Nonno. Neat! — Like the one Garibaldi wears in that
painting . . . his portrait."

Anthony nodded. "I wanted to keep warm, too. This snow may mean
business tonight." Then he grinned and added, "Not such an old fart, am I?
— And not crazy, like your father and the senior Salvaggi try to tell you."

"They don't tell me anything, Nonno, not about you." He paused to
take a deep breath and looked outside. "But can you drive well enough
to get us through everything? This stuff doesn't look so easy now. It's
thickening."

Anthony grinned. "The Maresciallos are canny and strong. We
know the outdoors — especially around here — like natives. Don't worry
about a thing."

The storm had started slowly, but gradually gathered force through the night. As Anthony drove out of town and Marcello felt the road beneath them lift more steeply into the mountains, he saw what looked like a huge white cloud descend toward the windshield, speckle the glass, and, through the rhythmic wipers, transform the twin cones of their headlights from yellow and beige to pure white gauze.

"Better slow down, Nonno," Marcello said.

Anthony waved, whistling. "I can see, my boy. With this four-wheel drive truck and good brakes, you don't have to worry about the roads."

But they watched a car spin on the opposite side of the road and crawled past a jack-knifed trailer in one of their own lanes. The cloud of snow surrounded the area completely now, turning the gauze outside into a soupy, thickened white fog that grew increasingly solid until it seemed they were riding through a creamy pool. Still Anthony drove on fearlessly, claiming the storm would pass over, until on the rising highway above them, miraculously, they saw a patch of clear dark ink with the half-round face of a yellow moon shining from it. "It's like a marble airplane," he said, pointing to the sky. "Or a flying marble saucer."

Anthony nodded. "These are the mountains. We're rising above the weather until we get to ours — Maresciallo's!"

Marcello grinned, listened to the soft mash of snow thrown off the tires against the chassis, and reached across the seat to pat his grandfather's muscular, reassuring thigh. He felt comfortable, confident, as he told the police later. They passed through another, harsher squall, climbed still higher until they saw no more tall trees; and then from a rocky plateau Anthony stopped and pointed to clear roads and moonlight on one part of the mountain while a black and gray cloud hung over another, the side the town lay under.

"It will stay that way," Anthony told him. "We're riding right on the storm line. Hills and mountains block the air currents, hold the clouds in place. But when we turn back toward town at the crossing, we'll find snow again. Not much, I hope. But you may have to hang on."

Marcello nodded, grinning. "I can if you can, Nonno."

Anthony smiled. "We're beyond it now. Hell, the only thing we have to worry about is keeping warm."

He was crazy, Jack thinks, whenever Marcello mentions that part of the evening now. Anthony knew the weather there. He knew they would likely get hit harder, by more than petty squalls. But to this day

Marcello refuses to believe it himself. "He may have misjudged things, but he really believed we would have an easy time of it," he says.

As Anthony turned off the highway and took the crossing back toward town, he probably still had no clear plan, according to Marcello. He was developing one as they drove. They were going somewhere to "sort things out" and then move on before anyone could find them; that is, before Margo finished her current research at Sunnyview, took Marcello and Tina back to school in New Hope, thereby canceling any chance for Anthony to negotiate the future through his son and grandson. But then this snow, rare, untimely, and unusually heavy for the time of the year, intervened.

It fell through the night — heavily. As they crawled along back roads toward town again, staying close to the river before reaching the backside of the mountain and following the small side road that ran up to and past the quarry, pellets of rain and ice mixed with the snow. The tires slipped at chancier places, once or twice carrying them close to the edge of an overhang. But Anthony reacted quickly, steering the car toward the inside lane without a moment's hesitation, never, according to Marcello, losing control. They could not see (at least Marcello couldn't), but Anthony insisted he could make out the road and the machines and trucks of the quarry itself. "Our past," he said, patting his chest and head as they rumbled near. "It's engraved, my boy, both here and here. Now it's sold, and the Salvaggi boys are going to start building."

They drove slowly onto the quarry grounds, then through the open back gate toward the top of another mountain beyond until they came to a second rocky area filled with brush, laurel, and small pine. They had parked there once or twice before, for hunting and observation. Anthony stopped next to a bushy enclosure; he and Marcello pulled dry wood, sleeping bags, and other equipment from the bed of the truck, carrying it into the enclosure where they constructed a lean-to and a small fire.

By this time the temperature had fallen into the low twenties, and in town, as the police, Franco, Jack, and Sonny waited to travel into the hills on the search, they wondered what conditions Marcello and Anthony endured. "Unseasonal precipitation," the TV weatherman said that night. "Here to stay, I'm afraid, perhaps for another couple of days."

Afterward, people praised Anthony, though reluctantly: he took care of his grandson first, they heard, wrapping him in a down sleeping bag, piling on his own heavy sheepskin coat, and throwing another sleeping bag on top of that while he, wearing only a heavy wool sweater and jacket, worked to keep the small fire going through the night. When he grew tired or cold, he climbed under the sheepskin coat and lay next to Marcello on the ground cloth, but he allowed the boy to keep both sleeping bags for warmth.

Miraculously, he survived at eighty-five, not even getting frostbite that first night, perhaps, some biologist at the university theorized, because piled snow provided effective natural insulation, like an igloo. In town wind blew it into drifts seven or eight feet high, breaking a fifty year record, while, toward morning, as the sky lightened and the atmosphere warmed, more freezing rain fell, topping everything with a hard, icy crust. On the mountain, according to Marcello's description afterward, it felt much worse. Wind blew bitterly through the lean-to, and the paltry fire did little more than keep the snow from piling too high at the opening.

Yet, Marcello said, they both slept soundly, waking at dawn to a brooding purple sky and a surrounding landscape covered, not with snow, Marcello reported to the local media, but with what seemed like gray, iridescent ash. "Like a volcano," Marcello whispered, "like pictures I've seen of Vesuvius after it erupts."

"This is the world, boy," Anthony said in the middle of it, adding more wood and kindling to the embers of their fire. "This is where man, especially a Maresciallo, shows his worth."

But even Marcello recognized the impossibilities — for them that night, for his great grandfather, Carmine, many years before, and a whole legion of immigrants streaming across the ocean to the mountains to join him in building the town so long ago. Snow swamped everything, the lean-to, the laurel, transforming their pickup into a fifteen-foot camel's hump of purple-gray. With all the engine power, Marcello knew, with all the four-wheel drives in the county and maybe the world, they would never move that vehicle, much less transport themselves from the mountain to another, safer site.

"It's beautiful, Nonno," Marcello murmured, crawling out of his sleeping bag for a closer look that morning. He shivered happily, rubbing his arms and shoulders with gloved hands as he stood next to his grandfather and stared out. Beyond the enclosure the snow made a mountainous landscape of its own, inhibiting the wind, of course, but also blocking any way out or in by foot. With a lump in his throat, Anthony must have sensed an ending there. Through the years he had heard the stories everyone else in town knew: climbers trapped on ledges, unable to descend, freezing to death or near death overnight; experienced hikers misjudging the weather, underestimating the severity or speed of a storm and not being rescued, or unable to come down themselves, for days. The most famous and romantic: a pair of lovers, found naked, still trying to embrace in death under all their gear and two or three feet of snow. But as Anthony must have guessed, this storm was worse than anything the county had experienced during his lifetime. In town nothing, not even SUV's, got through. By the middle of the previous month, drivers had removed snowtires from their cars; the Pennsylvania Department of Transportation had stripped plows from their trucks. And because of the lack of preparedness, the whole mountain area stayed home or indoors for three full days: utility company trucks, private cars, even the police. Mail stopped, the newspaper did not publish except on webpages, and journals from out of town never arrived. Officials depended on the Internet and ham radio operators to keep in touch with New York, Philadelphia, and Harrisburg.

Meanwhile, in the mountains Anthony must have battled his secret doubts. His last opportunity to influence the future of the family line stood beside him, and he had led not only himself and the boy, but all of the Maresciallos to this potential ending. With all the will in the world, he knew they could not move through that snow.

They cooked breakfast — powdered eggs, coffee, bread — and then quickly began to secure themselves against more weather. They took camp shovels and piled snow at one end of the lean-to as well as on the lean-to itself. Marcello stood on Anthony's shoulders to build a ten-foot wall around the enclosure, and then on hands and knees, he burrowed a tunnel toward the truck, handing snow in bucketfuls back to Anthony, who remained in the enclosure. Luckily, the sun shone beautifully — and warm — melting surface snow, although air temperatures stayed well below freezing through the day. They ate lunch, thought about dinner. And, at Anthony's suggestion, they had a snack of bread and potatoes while going to sleep. Before driving up there, Anthony probably counted on living off the wild for food. He and Marcello could have hunted and fished in better weather, and Anthony knew from his reading what plants to eat. But snow covered everything, animals, birds, and plants or water. They could not see anything, not the river, not the nearby lakes, not the turkey buzzards and hawks that regularly soar along the Delaware, and certainly no rabbits or squirrels.

They slept from sundown that night to well-past dawn, preserving as much energy as possible. Anthony worried about the fire, the little food they possessed, their limited supply of wood and matches. He still lay beside the boy, wearing nothing more than a sweater, corduroys, boots, and gray wool socks. He compromised by lying closer, dangerously close, Marcello said, to the fire.

By the second morning his feet had turned blue and his hands, cupped between his thighs through the night, had started to lose feeling. Marcello reported that his face had turned dull and ashen, the same color, he remarked, as the snow in the purple dawn light. Anthony trembled as the boy attempted to warm him with rekindled fire. They made coffee and powdered eggs, eating their last loaf of bread. "Grandpop was very somber at that," Marcello told his father afterward. But both their spirits picked up around noon — after they saw a plane fly over the mountain. It was the first human sign since they had driven out of town.

Marcello tunneled to the truck again, cleared around it, and then, slowly through the afternoon, shoveled snow off its roof. Weak, Anthony remained alone in the lean-to, wrapped in down and sheepskin, calling out to the boy every few minutes. They heard two more planes fly overhead. Then they spotted a pair of crows nearby but could not coax them into good shooting range. After Marcello cleaned off the truck, he started the engine, led Anthony on a crawl through the tunnel, and for more than an hour, he told police, sat with his grandfather in the heated cab and listened to Philadelphia music and news.

Search parties had started after them already. By afternoon state police and marshals flew in helicopters along the river and close to the mountains, searching for stranded campers. Jack had given the police a description of the truck, the boy, and the man, also telling them Anthony's favorite spots for hunting around the quarry. Margo, Tina, and Sonny waited at Franco's house as Jack went out with the state police, and Franco made frequent trips down the road to visit Mary. He found her lying in bed, listening to the radio while the nurse, Rosalie Amato, sat nearby. Margo stayed in touch with the police, but talked to no one but her daughter. She paced from window to window in the Salvaggi living room, fingered one of Sonny's cigars, and occasionally flicked it against her teeth without lighting it. She looked fragile, separated from her emotions, obviously finding it difficult to talk without crying and obviously wanting to protect her daughter from fear. Sonny tried to commiserate, tell her, as he had several times in recent years, how much he thought of her and her little family, but Margo's grim, serious expression warned him away.

He admitted to Franco that he believed, as Franco and everyone else did as a matter of fact, that Marcello and Anthony were dead already, or near it, if they had not made it through the mountains during the storm. Margo refused to consider the thought, as Sonny could see, pursing her lips stubbornly, biting angrily on her knuckles from time to time, gnawing her cuticles or nails before embracing Tina and staring into the distance as they listened to police radio calls or heard Franco and Roseanna pick up the phone to call for the latest news. To Sonny, Margo seemed to take the storm and its power personally. When, on the second day of waiting, Jack tramped through the room with his shoulders bowed and his head down as he slumped into the sofa cushions, she bristled around him and swung her arms near his head.

"Can't you do anything?" she said, as he lay back and closed his eyes. "You look so . . . defeated."

Jack said nothing, his eyes opened narrowly in anger, as he stared at his feet.

"Can't you do anything . . . useful? It's your son."

"Margo, I'm doing what I can. Everyone in town is. It doesn't look so good out there."

She shook her head.

"It doesn't look so good in here, either," she answered.

He looked at her back, sighing. "We're in this together, you know. I'm the wrong person to fight about it."

Margo spread her arms and clenched her fists, as if in fact she were ready to strike him at that moment. Sighing, Jack looked past her toward Tina. The young girl smiled.

"Come on, show some courage," Margo said. "We've been through worse than this together. I want to —"

She stopped, turning in frustration toward Sonny, who had just entered the room with a cup of coffee. Jack looked at him too and said nothing.

Margo had begun to show some age by this time, especially around the waist and thighs, but the added two or three pounds gave her a hardy, healthful appearance. She still looked fierce, strong, and at the moment had peered up at the heavens, as if to say this whole experience was unfair to her. Why did it have to snow that night in this place — and so heavily? Why hadn't the normal spring warmth melted it away?

Jack remained on the couch and leaned back, trying to rest his eyes. He had worked with the police through two full nights by now, sleeping only an hour or two and subsisting on occasional cups of coffee or food that Roseanna, Margo, or Rosalie brought to him. He had called all the hotels, inns, and motels in and around the mountains. He had flown up in the police helicopter over the gap and seen nothing of Marcello or Anthony, although he helped rescue another man and boy stuck on an overlook across the river. By car, snowmobile, and foot, he explored the fields behind Franco's house, Anthony's house, his own cabin, and the place where Margo and Tina stayed, as well as portions of the mountains along the Appalachian Trail. He flew over the quarry as well, staring at old, rusted machines caught in the snow like stranded, frozen cattle, and then past them to the top of the family mountain where Anthony and Marcello's enclosure lay. But, like everyone else, he saw nothing. "No smoke," he muttered to Margo when he returned. "There's too much wind. And with the snow piled so high, they're afraid we'll have to wait until the thaw to find them."

"Thaw?" Margo shook her head. "How long will that be?"

Jack raised his eyebrows, shrugging. "Snow covers everything up there."

Margo sighed. "Jack, Marcello is out there — alive." Her face turned whiter as she glared at him.

"So's my dad," he said, grimly.

She frowned. "You have to do everything you can. Jack, you can't let him . . . them —"

He shook his head as Margo slumped down into a chair. In the far corner, Tina stared at her mother warily. "We've done everything," Jack said. "Now we're doing stuff again. I just hope the truck got through the mountains, and they headed someplace else."

"Marcello may be suffering," Margo said, shaking. "In this cold, he —" She stopped, went to Tina in the corner, and put her arms around her. Her hand went helplessly to her forehead. Her shoulders hunched forward as she shivered and looked out the window to the road.

"My friends," Sonny said, "maybe we can —"

She whirled on him, holding Tina's head close to her chest as she spoke. "Sonny, this is between Jack and me — for once. I'm here because of him — and that sick blind man he calls his father."

Jack laughed, but with absolutely no humor behind it.

"Please —" Sonny said, reaching toward her. "Consider better possibilities. Anthony knows the mountains — especially around the quarry. He's been going up there his whole life."

"That won't do him any good, Sonny," Jack said. "Especially in this weather. He'd have to drive through it." He shook his head.

A yellow PennDoT truck rumbled by. Its plow hurled a spume of snow on top of the drift on the opposite side of the road. For a moment, the living room window rattled, and they all looked up as if suddenly jarred awake. Imagining the snow as water now, Jack saw it covering every tree and landscape feature in sight. Anthony — and, of course, Marcello — had to be worrying and wondering at that moment. As the PennDOT truck ground its way around the curve higher up the hill, all three heard its chains slip and slide on the ice and then a loud bang as it suddenly shifted weight and hit a tree or rock on the roadside.

"Somebody will get through all right," Jack said. "But we have a very important problem of time."

"They'll make it. I know Marcello will make it," Margo said. She looked deeply into Tina's eyes, then hugged her again and stared up at the ceiling. "Somebody must get through. They've got to. . . ."

She shook her fists, tossing her head in frustration, and tears welled up in her eyes as Tina pulled away and looked up at her. "Mama," she said. "I want my brother."

She turned to Sonny, to Jack, and with a sudden spasm of a sob, covered her face, falling heavily against Margo's chest. As soon as Sonny stepped near, Margo raised her hands to block him. "The man is obsessed. The man is obsessed enough to pull down his own family — even his grandchild — with him."

Sonny looked at her, trying for a comforting smile. "He may be crazy, Margo, but I'm sure he wants to keep Marcello alive."

Jack glanced up but said nothing as Sonny touched her shoulder and caressed Tina's hair.

"They're both tough and stubborn," Jack said. "It's in our family blood."

28.

Margo did not even smile at that. Instead, she lifted Tina in her arms and took her out into the kitchen to be with Roseanna. After a few moments, the two women walked through the living room and up the stairs, each holding one of little Tina's hands. When Margo came down half an hour later, she had clenched her fists again, but took the handkerchief Sonny offered her and stared across the room at Jack. He had closed his eyes once more, overwhelmed with sleeplessness and worry. Due to go up in the helicopter again later that afternoon, he wondered what they would find. Probably nothing good. Soon the phone rang and all three sat erect together, listening in silence as, upstairs, Roseanna answered. They stared into the center of the room, at each coupling of their six spread-out feet, the carpet, and finally the legs of a table and chair. After a few moments, Roseanna walked halfway down the stairs, and, her soft face just below the landing, leaned forward giving a little, weary grin.

"Important?" Sonny said, trying not to look too apprehensive.

Roseanna nodded, gravely.

"My god, what is it?"

Margo rose, stepped toward the stairway, and together Jack and Sonny stood like parents waiting for word about a child.

"Smoke," Roseanna said, looking down at Jack.

"Smoke?"

She shook her head and shrugged. "In the mountains. The wind's calmed. They're flying up to take a look in about an hour."

Jack left immediately, going out the door with his coat already on, and jogging down the snow-covered walkway to his old car before Margo and Sonny had a chance to ask about circumstances. Soon they left too, going behind Sonny's apartment to Margo's SUV and driving past the main house onto the road toward town. Jack had headed directly for the emergency helicopter landing pad beside the county hospital, assuming the state police would stop there for medical supplies before flying into the mountains. With main roads mostly cleared by now, he arrived fairly quickly, in time to help load supplies onto the copter. Then he climbed into the craft and, wearing a helmet, with a set of field glasses in his hands, took a seat and watched the pilot and co-pilot start the engine. It caught immediately, the blades sputtering at first before gathering speed and gradually building to an ear-splitting roar above them. They fastened their seatbelts. The pilot closed the door and with a nod toward Jack prepared to leave just as Margo's car arrived with Sonny's hand out the passenger window waving his hat.

Margo leaped from the car, her mouth open wide in a silent scream, and ran through the parking lot toward the helicopter. Sonny limped after, leaning on his cane, still waving his hat awkwardly as he stumbled behind her.

"Please, please!" Jack read on her lips. "I. . . . Marcello's mother."

But neither the pilot nor co-pilot heard her above the blades' body-shaking roar, although they could have guessed immediately and accurately, as Jack had, what she was saying. He tapped the pilot's shoulder and nodded, the co-pilot opened the door, and, just before lifting off, he and Jack leaned out to help Margo and the hobbling Sonny in.

Years afterward Sonny still remembered and described the views during the flight, his first ever above the town. The landscape looked gentle, white to bluish gray in the sun, like a faded cotton blanket on which they looked for smudges of man-made smoke or light. The machines at the quarry, snow-locked, had not moved around the piles of sand and slate for at least a year. No one had cleaned or driven up the roads that far, and so from the air the surrounding mountain seemed to have exploded, throwing up an eerie frozen tinder in a helter-skelter fashion. It smothered everything, including the Maresciallo quarry, smoothing out and leveling hills, leaving no safe haven for the copter to land in outside of town.

But the machine rose above it, flew along what once had been the access road for Maresciallo's, hovered past felled trees, rusted buildings, and white-covered rock-face to where the brush and mountain laurel showed through the whitish gray as nothing more than occasional freaky green blotches. They observed no smoke or fire and, awful for Margo, Jack, and Sonny, not a sign of human movement as they rose and fell here and there along the mountain's side. The pilot dipped close to the snow, ascended quickly because he feared the sudden strong currents that blew along the mountaintop, and then, as they moved north and east toward the Delaware, dipped toward the ground again, this time near a hill of snow through which some brush showed, as if it were some timber holding up a tee-pee.

"Down there," the co-pilot blurted. He looked through his glasses and pointed. "I saw smoke there earlier. It must be somebody still. . . ."

The pilot dropped closer, circled to the other side of the structure (piled brush, they saw, with a flimsy lean-to in the middle), and then about twenty-five or thirty feet beyond that Jack made out his father's truck: black, shining, reflecting the blue sky and clouds above it. One door opened. A small figure, thick-limbed, stepped into the sun and waved. Margo gave a start and shouted. They saw jeans, a tan sheepskin coat hanging from the shoulders, and a brown hat with earflaps, all so big they seemed to weigh the wearer down. "It's Marcello," Margo whispered. "Thank God, it's him." Tears welled from her eyes. Silent, Jack and Sonny nodded.

They saw Marcello cup his hands around his mouth then wave. Puffs of white breath indicated he was shouting. He leaped up and down, gesturing behind him as the snow, whipped up by the copter blades, blew into his face and past him in a feathery motion toward the truck. "No place to land," the pilot said. As the copter dipped lower and the co-pilot let the rope ladder out rung by rung, another figure, larger, stiffer, lumbering, slowly emerged from the truck. Even from a distance, Anthony looked terrible, Sonny thought. He wore no jacket, coat, or hat, his bald head and face glowing ashen gray in the light. He did not wave, as Marcello had. He did not jump or open his mouth. Grimly, he reached up, took the bottom of the ladder with his left hand, and then gave the boy a boost on his right hand and knee until he could hook the toe of his foot on the lowest rung. Now Marcello's hat flew to the ground and scuttled along the crust of the blowing snow. He seemed to cry out as he climbed, but in the copter they understood nothing until, shivering on the top rung, he threw his leg into the craft, took the first hand offered to him, Margo's, and fell heavily into his mother's arms. She shouted, her voice tearful and hoarse. Then a sudden shift in weight and wind lifted the helicopter up and away from the car.

"Mom! Dad! No! Don't leave yet! We've got to get him. We've

got to go after Grandpa!"

Marcello squirmed free, pushing and elbowing toward the door.

"Easy, Marcello, easy. We'll go back for him," Jack said, embracing him and holding him down.

Marcello shivered now in Jack's arms. The co-pilot passed Margo a blanket and began to pour hot liquid from a thermos. Marcello pushed both cup and blanket away.

"You've got to hurry!" he shouted. "You've got to go back — down for him — now!" He pointed toward the truck.

Squirming free again, Marcello lunged for the door and reached for the handle.

"Easy, Marcello, easy! We'll take care of him." Jack patted his hand, grasped his shoulders, and held on tightly. They all saw the young boy tremble.

"Can't you see? We're going to lower now," the co-pilot shouted. "We'll bring him up."

"But we have to go down for him! We have to bring him up! He can't — He won't —"

Jack embraced him, trying to keep him quiet. But Marcello struggled against his grip and, once again, dived for the door. As he reached it, pushing it open, Jack caught his ankle, and a gust of wind tipped the copter toward the opposite side. They all rolled in that direction, lurching with the aircraft, and Sonny and the co-pilot clinged to their seatbelts to keep from falling. The pilot cursed, maneuvering to right the craft, and the co-pilot, bracing himself while shouting, shoved Marcello into Jack's arms and pulled the door shut.

"Nonno's going to be all right, Marcello! He's going to be all right! Don't you see?" Jack pointed through the window toward the truck.

"But he won't — He doesn't want to leave — I tell you he doesn't!"

"What?" the co-pilot said. He looked at Jack.

"He doesn't want to come up, I tell you! He says he won't."

Sonny and Margo looked through the window now. The ground grew closer, but they no longer saw Anthony beneath the aircraft. The snow turned gray as the shadow of the blades and ship spread over the truck, the tee-pee, and the lean-to. With unearthly effort it seemed, the helicopter hovered, blades and engine roaring, the wind kicking up fresh snow that began to cover the truck. They rose slowly, circled the mountaintop and returned watching, still not finding a safe place to land.

By the time they turned toward the hospital again (Marcello, shivering, babbling hysterically, needed immediate care, Margo insisted), Anthony had disappeared completely. Like a giant, gray mound of ash, blowing snow was all. The mountaintop looked wasted, desolate. As Jack said when he described it for the newspapers afterward, it was as if no one — human, animal, or vegetable — had ever lived, breathed, or eaten there. "Likely," one of the reporters quoted, "no one ever would."

29.

For years, whenever he visited his father, Marcello slept in Jack's old room in the Maresciallo house and, placing a small, portable cassette recorder between them on Anthony's walnut desk, invited Sonny to come over and talk about various things: their families, the Garibaldi Club and Sunnyview, which Sonny had built, Carmine Maresciallo, who had supplied the brick and stone, and, of course, Italy because it had supplied everything else.

Sonny felt reluctant about the whole project, even though he knew Marcello did it for good cause. He had visited Italy many times, searching his own family origins, and had come up with little. His father, Giovanni Battaglia, according to his mother, had never surfaced and likely never would. Meanwhile, Modestina's ancestry remained shrouded under years and years of paper records that had either burned or been hopelessly lost beneath the rubble of war or one of the violent earthquakes that shook the Potenza region from time to time. Memory? — Sonny had very little to go on there. His mother had refused to tell him much, and his own mind, he admitted, grew increasingly numb. At first he took a hint from his mother and refused to talk about himself or his experiences, not wanting to be treated as a statistic for some college professor, or revisit sad, bitter times like a nostalgic, grouchy old man. But then Marcello bought the little digital camcorder, and Sonny, seeing how important it was to the young man, had second thoughts.

"This is for our history," Marcello said, "not just for a professor." He set up a small plastic tripod before Sonny and attached a miniature Flip recorder to it. "Tell me, what was happening at the beginning of last century? With Carmine as well as your mother — all the Maresciallos and Salvaggis. What do you think were their intentions in coming here?"

"Intentions?" Sonny laughed, rubbing his thumb and fingers above the table. "We all came here to make a better living."

"Carmine and your father? All the people before them, right back to the beginning?"

"Carmine was first," Sonny said. "It's the Italian trap, from Columbus forward. We all think America will make us rich."

"Hey, why not? That's part of the baggage on our shoulders."

Sonny shook his head, ticking off main points on his right hand. "He was a great navigator — the best of his time — and an entrepreneur who convinced a foreign king to fund his project. Be proud of that business sense. He landed in a brand new world — by design or not — that brought new life to exiles like my mother and everyone who came after — including today. Forget the suffering natives — thousands, maybe millions of southern Italians made up for that when they came here to work for practically nothing! Baggage, Marcello? — I'd say it's carrying us rather than the other way around."

They travelled back together one spring, Sonny, Jack, Marcello, the Flip recorder too, of course, and also an old tape recorder that Sonny brought. They flew to Geneva, Sonny carrying his mother's ashes with him. She had died nearly two years before, well on her way to one hundred. On her own and unattended, no longer in touch with the outside world, she refused help from Sonny, Franco, or anyone else. A pension, some savings, just a few extra dollars here and there from Sonny, and a grit that made her insist on caring for herself right to the bitter, lonesome end: no nurses, no doctor, no charity, and certainly no barbiturates. She could read, and she could walk. For years she wheeled her groceries home from the neighborhood supermarket, not far from her downtown apartment, where she insisted on living despite pleas from Sonny and Franco to try the professional comforts of Sunnyview.

"I don't need that," she argued, "even if it's free. When I can't live by myself, I want to die."

"Nonna," Franco pleaded. "With all due respect, you are getting too old for independence."

"I will know when I am ready for your help!" she shouted. "If I ever am!"

"There are people your own age there, men and women you can talk to. Nurses, doctors, me. . . ."

Modestina shook her head. "I talk to no one. My friends, my experiences are all up here. Quiet, like my memories."

Franco, and Sonny too, looked at her stern face and said nothing. Her world, as well as most of her memories, much to Sonny's regret, remained there, born up in smoke toward the sky when she, in a terse rejection of her early Roman Catholic training, told Sonny on her deathbed that she wanted no coffin, no burial, certainly no embalming fluid, and simply wanted her body wrapped in the two contrasting flags of her personal history, the red, white and green of Italy, the red, white, and blue of the United States, and set to flame as soon as legally possible after her last breath.

"No mourning, no funeral, no donation of body parts," she ordered, her voice clear and, to Sonny's mind, absolute. "I want to go back entirely, replenish the earth I came from with everything I took upon first seeing the light."

Sonny had tried to do as she demanded, although not quite knowing what to make of her last wishes, especially the "replenish the earth I came from" part. How specific was the spot she wanted to replenish? And "first seeing the light"? What did that mean? — Potenza (the street, the town, her actual birth house)? Italy in general? Perhaps the planet Earth, having nourished her on two major continents? Or was it America, Pennsylvania, and Maresciallo's Mountain where Modestina, a reborn *Americana* Modestina, with a different destiny from the former Italian one, found a prosperous, if somewhat lonesome, vision of life's new possibilities?

The urn of ashes sat on a shelf next to Sonny's bed for more than a year. Meanwhile he and Franco debated her last wish. Franco thought they should set the urn in a family plot in a beautiful corner somewhere on the Salvaggi property. "Give her a cozy corner with a beautiful view of the river, or the mountains to the west," he ventured. "This is her true home. She worked and sweated for it, along with you."

But Sonny thought she had been too independent for that. He had sensed urgency in Modestina's last words that gave a very fundamental meaning to her wish to return to the very earth that had nurtured her. "Potenza," Marcello whispered to Sonny when they discussed it one summer afternoon, "and as close to the house she was born in as possible." He was a history major in college by then, and the sense of origins excited him.

Sonny discussed it with several people, and in the end he supported a Pennsylvania burial, but with a slight alteration: "The two flags mean something," he said to Franco. "Give her back to both places: Italy and Pennsylvania. Each one nourished her."

The idea appalled Franco, who called it a division of her soul, but appealed to Marcello and Jack. At first Sonny held firm, but he found he could not bring himself to lift the urn's lid, much less look inside and divide its contents in two. During one stormy evening alone, he swore he heard howling voices in the wind when he stood in the yard, and for several nights afterward imagined his mother's severe, pale face looming before him in the dark. Sonny quickly turned on the outside lights.

One fall afternoon he decided to settle it once and for all. With Marcello, Jack, and Franco as company, he scattered a third of the urn's contents on the old footpath up Maresciallo's Mountain and a third on the banks of the Delaware River beneath it. As a kind of memorial, he placed the nearly empty urn on the shelf next to his bed for another six months when, finally, after speaking to Franco, he decided to travel to Italy to finish the job. Franco begged off because of duties at Sunnyview, but Marcello and then Jack offered to go with him. "We'll fly into Switzerland," Sonny said, "then drive through the mountains into Italy, follow the boot into Potenza, and leave the rest of her there."

Marcello nodded.

"Her people were peasants: miners, farmers."

"Raw. Unfinished," Jack said. "Just like my grandfather."

"*Cafoni*," Sonny said, "just like Giovanni, whoever he may be."

30.

Before the trip, Sonny asked Marcello — now a bright student getting ready for graduate school — to read the packet of papers Anthony had left especially for him and that Sonny had wanted to carry along with Modestina's ashes to Italy. He had found them several years before, a letter, notes, one or two unfinished essays and poems, stuffed in a manila envelope the mail carrier dropped on Sonny's doorstep four days after the snowstorm ended. Puzzled, Sonny had opened the packet, hastily read part of it, and, angered at a couple of the things he saw, carried it all, unmentioned to anyone, into Franco's attic, where he threw them into a cold, dusty corner. He did not open the envelope again until a week before the flight to Europe.

"It's a treasure trove of his thoughts," he told Marcello. "But not a word — not one goddamn meaningful word! — about anything important, to you or me!"

"Maybe that's a life-saver," Jack said. "Who would want to read it? He must have been crazy."

Marcello shrugged, aimed the small camcorder toward Sonny, and motioned toward the recorder on the seat beside him. "But my great, great grandfather Carmine is in it, I'll bet."

"Warts and all," Sonny answered. "Especially the warts."

Marcello nodded. "M-m-m. Let's begin with that. You knew him. What kind of man was he? My father won't say."

"*Can't* say," Jack said. "I don't remember much, except how hard he used to pinch my cheek when he saw me." He grimaced. "It still hurts."

Sonny nodded, turning from the camcorder to Jack, whose broad back hunched over his hands, meaty with middle age now, gripping the steering wheel. They drove the highway south of Rome, on their way to Potenza at this time.

"What kind of man could he have been?" Sonny said. "*Mezzo, mezzo* — like everyone. But Carmine started our county, and —" Sonny shook his hand, as if to test a doorknob with his fingers. "And he was always good to me. Your grandfather thought he was too good because he helped me start in business — the building business."

"Only the start?" Jack said.

"He even wanted to turn the quarry over to me at one point. He didn't trust Anthony to run it, but your Grandmother Carmella — and my mother — wouldn't let him. My mother said I should make a living on my own, and I did."

Marcello nodded. "Tell me about them," he said. "Carmine and Carmella."

"Turn off the camera — and the tape recorder," Sonny said. "First look at your grandfather's notes. He knew as much — or more — than

I did. Pretty soon at my age, I won't be able to read them myself. It will be enough to worry about keeping warm."

Marcello patted Sonny's shoulder and sighed. He turned off the two recorders and pointed to a dry, rocky landscape with cone-shaped, volcanic mountains bunched on the horizon. The flattened, jagged tops and brown scars flashing through the brush reminded each of them of home — the harsh, ragged lines, the burnt wood and gray ash Anthony had created so spectacularly in Pennsylvania that late spring evening when Marcello was still a boy.

As they marveled at the Mezzogiorno landscape that afternoon, each remembered the earlier spring and the inventory of equipment the State Police found around Anthony's pickup: spools of wire, sticks of dynamite, a ticking clock, and, almost anachronistic, a hand detonator. Lastly, under a pile of darkened, ash-covered snow, the Garibaldi hat, frozen stiff, like a Hollywood prop for a final image. Considering what they had found inside the blood-spattered cab and bed of the truck — three shovels, a pick, surveyor's tools, and a shotgun — Anthony's, wrapped within his corpse's arms — it became clear what he intended to do up there. Headlines today would call him a terrorist, but then he was merely old and insane, especially at the Garibaldi Club where, with a young boy, possibly his last issue, riding along, no one harbored a doubt.

"What could have driven him?" the local newspaper editorial asked. "What immigrant's grudge?"

"He was American! He had no immigrant's grudge!" Sonny shouted each time he read the question. "He hated everything. The bastard wanted to blow us all up!"

He shot out his fist and slapped his biceps with his other hand.

"It was an obscene salute!" he bellowed, over and over again down at the Garibaldi Club. "For everyone!"

No one could prove, or understand, anything of Anthony's motives, and now, on the road toward Naples, for perhaps the thousandth time in the intervening years, Marcello and Sonny reviewed the details of the explosions: three sudden, separate bursts of light then succeeding, what-seemed-like, sudden sonic booms, chunks of concrete, snow, and metal hurtling from the peaks at the town's horizon filling the sky before turning and raining down on everything close. Trees around the quarry trembled and leaned, quickly uprooted; small ponds and larger lakes all at once brimmed with mounds of soil and wood. Everyone at the club that day looked up and saw, or felt, a miracle: the sun shined one moment and then just disappeared. Finally, the mountain itself, or what little remained of it, changed into a shocking, black smoked memory after less than one quarter of an hour.

"Months," the police chief said to one reporter. "Maybe years — it had to take that long for such an elderly man to set up that dynamite and those wires alone. People thought he was hunting up there. But he was plotting."

Marcello sighed when he read that. Now, in Italy, he looked toward his father and hoped to hear forgiveness. He remembered lying dazed in the county hospital when the quarry blew, hardly even hearing the first couple of explosions. What he recalled vividly from the day's stirred, agitated dreams was the rattle of the windows and the chink-chink-chink of the water glass against a clay flower pot of geraniums his mother had brought in to cheer him up. On the highway from Pennsylvania to New York in recent years, he never escaped remorse over the brick villas and condos rising above the road — small rust-colored Monopoly blocks filling the scars of a mountain once predominantly granite, soil, and wood. Even with the three huge generating windmills churning above everything, the scene bothered him because "Uncle" Sonny's company had put it there.

"The storm intervened," the police chief said to a reporter. "He must have planned for a couple of years to take that quarry with him. His grandson became a privileged, unwitting witness. Or maybe he wanted to take him too."

Marcello denied that immediately. "We were supposed to drive through," he said to anyone who listened. "The snow came on us too fast. I can't believe he ever wanted to harm me — or the mountain. He meant to force the owners of the quarry to cancel the sale to Sunnyview Construction."

At the time no one believed him, especially the police, but Jack showed real sympathy for Marcello's argument. "There were other things going on," he had told one reporter. "I know my father loved his grandson and would never have wanted to harm him."

So the puzzle remained, with various prominent members of town and the Italian community taking different sides. A sociologist from the university published a paper on southern Italian immigration and used the explosion as an example of ethnic tensions coming to the fore; a historian and a young environmentalist from New Jersey joined to write a history of the vanished mountain and the town. One or two local singers wrote songs to make Anthony a kind of outlaw hero fighting for the land. But the key, most people puzzled over, was that he included Marcello in his plans.

"We talked about it," Marcello told investigators, "almost daily for a couple of weeks. But it was always playful, boyish discussion. How could we get a company like Sonny's to think about the mountain and its original people? We even joked about it on the way up that night."

"Joked?" Sonny had said, seeing, and not seeing, two landscapes beyond the hospital window, one designed and organized, the other full of wild, organic growth. "He should have driven to New Jersey with his grandson and blown up the mountain later. He — and the boy — should have been home free — and safe."

Marcello shook his head when the reporter looked at him: "He didn't want me to go back to New Hope with my mother. He wasn't seeing —"

"Seeing? He wanted you with him, even in death," Sonny had shouted. "He wanted to prove to you he could defeat me."

Marcello looked toward the floor beside his bed. Years later, in Italy, he looked out another window and saw a line of jagged river rock along a shallow stream beside the car. Occasionally he heard the tired downturn of defeat in Sonny's voice, and sometimes, once or twice during this trip, even in his father's. Fatigue, worry, age, or destiny. Were they each following the path of others in their town? — Lina, Anthony, Lillian, even Carmine, the founder, and Carmella? Flesh.

"Probably he wanted a witness," Jack had offered to the reporter. "Maybe it was a sentimental way of saying good-bye to a place he didn't want to lose. Marcello could enjoy it with him one last night. It was a pretty simple plan — until the freak snowstorm surprised him."

"Never," Sonny said, bitterly, although inside he conceded the possibility.

Jack clinged to his view, and years later, staring up at the hills and mountains of southern Italy, he would do the same, ever ready to allow his father's human weakness to stand. He heard Marcello start the recorder again and knew his son, much more like his mother than him, was ready to hear more. For his benefit, he tapped his finger on the dashboard, and, lowering his voice, repeated the question people had asked so many years before: "But what if he made a mistake in the wiring? Or mistimed the explosions? People make mistakes. Why would he risk his grandson's life?"

Sonny frowned. "He was crazy. People love the land. Look what they do."

He glanced at Marcello, who nodded his head and stared at the road. "My grandfather. . . ."

"Your grandfather was absolutely mad, my boy. Just as your father said. Probably from jealousy; or guilt — for selling off his father's land. Take it as a twisted compliment that he wanted you there."

Sonny reached over the seat, grasped Marcello's shoulder, then with his other hand tousled his hair. The skin just above his temples felt flush, softly resilient. "You think he loved you, my boy? Well, I'm sure he did. We all do."

He pinched Marcello's earlobe.

The young man said nothing. He had assured the police back home, as he had assured Sonny and Jack countless times on this trip, that Anthony had been in full control: calm, lucid, most of all, kind. In the lean-to he spoke primarily of keeping Marcello warm and finding enough food to eat.

"He said nothing about the quarry? Nothing about blowing the whole mountain, with his family name on it, off the map?"

Marcello frowned. "For a joke, I told you, to keep our minds off the storm. He said he'd blow up everything right then if it would do any good. But the time wasn't right: Snow would keep falling, and they'd line up subdivisions as soon as they ploughed through. In less than a year, he said, it would look like a suburban skyline. He was nearly right."

Sonny swallowed, wincing as Jack nodded and Marcello looked away. He motioned toward the mountains on the right side of the road and turned his camcorder in that direction. The sky shone blue above them but, despite the clarity, day had started to darken already. Ahead, Vesuvius squatted like a tired wild animal, its smoke rising lazily in the distance. Windows across from it shimmered with man-made light.

"I wanted to buy that quarry twenty years before," Sonny said, "to continue Carmine's work. I thought I owed him that, Anthony wouldn't even consider my bid."

"He didn't trust anyone in town to care for that business — and especially the mountain," Jack said. "Especially me."

"Everyone thought you couldn't, or wouldn't, handle it," Sonny said. "Some of us thought Margo might —"

"My mother?" Marcello interrupted. "People thought that even then?"

"Business was just not your father's style. But it always seemed to be your mother's. Isn't that right, Jack?"

Jack said nothing, just twisted his neck, scratched it, and glanced across the road toward the volcano. Darkly gray and blue within its muddy, brownish tones, the jagged, flat-topped shape reminded him of his father. Strip mining, new visitors to the Garibaldi Club and Sunnyview said about the remains of Maresciallo's Mountain, and the older members just nodded. The Italian sunset burned a reddish-amber on the windshield, reflecting outside shale and exposed rock-face in the hazy distance. The three men stared at the fading images and said nothing.

"My father told me you really wanted to buy the mountain for yourself, Sonny. Put the Salvaggi name on it instead of ours, and then, after a few years, turn it into a townhouse development. He said you wanted to erase the Maresciallo name. Is that true?"

Sonny closed his eyes.

"He said you had your reasons," Jack said. "But he never mentioned why he was so sure."

"The man was crazy. Marcello, stop the god-damn camera and read some of those letters for me."

He held out the old manila envelope. Marcello shuffled his feet as if to speak but sighed instead. "I've read them all, Uncle Sonny. Or most of them. Franco let me go up there and look at them from time to time." He shook his head. "To tell you the truth, I didn't see anything new."

Sonny pushed the envelope across the seatback. "These are different. I've kept them hidden. They have the Salvaggis in them, if only for a couple of passages."

Marcello looked away. He took one soft blue, dog-eared notebook and began leafing through it. His camcorder lay on the seat.

"He was a good man," Marcello said. "I'm sure of that. But about you, my grandfather never seemed to have control. He told me that himself. Then you — Well, you —"

"Obviously not in control either," Jack interrupted, frowning. "Like two kids fighting for attention."

Sonny looked up into Jack's eyes, startled at the sight of them peering at him in the rearview mirror. He glanced toward Marcello but said nothing. Jack almost never showed anger, so the question meant something to him. If truth be known, Sonny might have confessed that, along with his mother's ghost, he had encountered Anthony's spirit too in recent months, not only in the notebook pages he kept re-reading, but here, in the concrete Italian world he rode and walked through daily. This very morning he had dreamed of Anthony razzing him, whistling eerily in the lonesome dawn as he tried to sleep. Sometimes, although he knew he would doubt it the moment he told someone, he seemed to spot Anthony's massive figure just around a corner, or in the half-lit doorway to a room. Silent, Anthony raised his fist, and there were nights even here when, like a ludicrously large, wingless bird, Anthony seemed to hover outside the hotel window and moan, as he had recently, in the center of Rome. It was a dirge, Sonny imagined, his own.

"My grandfather never got over one thing," Marcello said, "My grandmother, Lillian. Her loss."

"The beloved wife routine!" Sonny slammed his fist twice on the back of the driver's seat.

"Jesus, Sonny," Jack muttered. "That almost took us off the road."

Sonny closed his eyes. Opening a window, he lighted a cigar and tried to push away all the memories. Still, they burned and seemed to bubble up in his throat.

"Lillian," Sonny said to Marcello. "Anthony blamed your father for her death."

"And others," Jack added. "Don't forget the others."

Sonny nodded.

"And me. Anthony Maresciallo made himself, and everyone around him, miserable. Including his son — and his wife. Sometimes, Carmine did too. It was the family way. Never laugh. Never play or make a joke. Then they blamed the world for the gloom surrounding them. And, of course, they — especially Anthony — liked to blame me. The hired help, 'the bastard son,' he called me, breaking stone in the father's quarry."

"Bastard son?"

Sonny chewed his cigar, fitfully. His words hung in the air while he pounded the seat back with his fist again. Tires skidded on gravel as they felt the car swerve. Quickly, Jack shifted gears and, with a grind, pulled them toward the middle of the road.

"I'm sorry," Sonny whispered.

Marcello mumbled something to Jack, who looked into the mirror again — at Sonny — and nodded.

"You were there," Marcello said finally. "My grandfather also told me. Now, my father —"

"I've talked to you about this before," Jack said to Marcello. "We all lived there then, right in the same neighborhood. My mother, my father, and me. Sonny came by very often, by himself."

Sonny closed his eyes (a bad memory, he told himself), but then, slowly, very slowly, he felt his mind gather into the present, and he looked up.

"Lived there? Where do you mean?"

"Near the Garibaldi Club," Jack said, "the site of my mother's accident."

"My grandfather told me you were at the scene, Sonny. Saw it."

"Of course, I did! I never denied it — to Anthony, or anyone else. I admitted it to the police. Ask your father; I told them —"

"And?"

"And what? —"

Marcello shook his head.

"We all remember it," Jack said, "pretty clearly. We don't want to remember it."

"But — I've told you — many times. It wasn't my fault — or yours. It happened. One of those awful, awful turns of life."

Sonny sighed. Jack leaned on the steering wheel and struggled to guide it while Marcello shifted in his seat. Sonny had always said he had nothing to hide, never had with Lina or Lillian, despite a varied, "interesting life." He could talk openly about anything — work, family, women — and yet. . . . What could he really say, what words to genuinely absolve himself here? The day of Lillian's accident loomed in all their lives, even Marcello's — a silly, stupid quarrel between a man and a woman not even his wife. And it was only here — in southern Italy — along with

Anthony's papers beside him, that he partially understood the drama.

"You were there for other things too," Marcello said. "My grand-father said they were important things."

"I'm not sure *important*'s the right word," Jack said, raising his eye-brows. "He said you were having an affair, Sonny, and that you were going to stop it — that's really why she did it."

"Did it, Dad? It wasn't an accident?"

Marcello looked at his father, who nodded, then at Sonny, who said nothing. Jack focused on the road again, as if he wanted nothing to do with his last few remarks. He wore his hair short now and frequently poked his nose forward dramatically beneath his broad forehead. Roman, Marcello had decided that morning, even more than southern Italian; hardly Irish or Tuscan, like Lillian, at all.

"He thought I was his brother," Sonny blurted, "a half brother," but the sight of Jack's eyes studying him closely in the rearview mirror stopped him cold. He nodded to Marcello and whispered dramatically, "Your grandmother was leaving me! To go back to him! I couldn't — no, wouldn't — believe it, still can't, to this day! She didn't kill herself, she was saving Jack! As I, the only full grown man near them, should have been. Instead, I. . . ."

He shrugged, noticing Jack's quizzical smile in the mirror, and shook his head, smiling a little himself.

"'Important things' — is that what my grandfather meant?" Marcello asked.

"He thought I was his half-brother, a real challenge to his inheri-tance. But read the letter," Sonny whispered, "the notebooks, whenever you can! He thought I might take it all away — the bastard!"

Sonny stopped and drew a breath. Jack had pulled off the highway, and after a few turns they approached Naples on the winding Amalfi Drive. Sonny and Marcello were held silent by the beautiful bay. As the water opened before them, Jack followed the long, sharp curves of the mountain wall beside them. Sonny closed his eyes from time to time, remembering earlier drives along here, several times with Lina, once with another woman, regrettably never (except for the ashes he carried now) with his mother. It was the most breath-taking automobile descent he had ever seen, the very narrow causeway, hair-raising turns, the ex-pansive, almost ghostly, beauty of the bay, and finally the sheer drop into the blue-green eye of the water. As they rode toward the city, he watched Marcello lean across the seat, rest his knuckles on the back, then rap on the fingers of Sonny's outstretched hand.

"Home, old friend," Marcello said, as if calling him back from another reverie. In the distance, somewhere behind, Sonny thought he heard a door slam. A few seconds afterward an engine began to roar, its reverberating sound echoing theirs as they began to pick up speed.

"My grandfather said you were there, always there — especially before my father was born," Marcello said. "Could it be? —" He looked at Sonny, then at his father and, with another tap at Sonny's fingers, continued. "He told me you might have more meaning in my life than I or anyone could imagine."

"Meaning?" Jack said. "You mean blood?"

Marcello nodded. "That's his word, exactly — and he also talked about family connection. You know what he was trying to say, Sonny?"

Jack turned the car toward the bay, then looked into the mirror and shook his head.

"I tell you he was out of his mind, *pazzo*," Sonny shouted. "Study the notebooks."

"But he said you —" Marcello paused.

"My mother would have told me — I'm sure of it! I've been trying to prove it for years — Giovanni Battaglia!"

Jack said nothing; a massive tour bus had suddenly loomed on the hairpin curve before them and all three held their breath. A gray, vague luminescence of smoke from the volcano filtered through the windows. The motion of the car, especially as they inched between the bus and the barrier around the curve, made it difficult to talk.

"Uncle Sonny, were you and my. . . ."

"Say it straight, my boy. I'm not hiding anything, never will."

"It seems obvious, but I need an answer. Were you and my grandmother more than friends?"

Sonny shook his head. He held up one of Anthony's notebooks and waved it in Marcello's face. "I told your mother and father years ago, before you were born. I met Lillian from time to time — for a cup of coffee, and talk. I was busy with work, unhappy with a lovely, drinking wife. Lillian was unhappy, too, with an angry, bitter husband. We needed each other — for talk. That's all."

"Intimate talk?" Marcello asked, blushing.

Sonny reached over the seat and dropped the notebook into Marcello's lap. He extended his thumb and little finger in front of his mouth, wagging them. "That was all! I assure you, I am more puzzled by my own parentage than yours."

Marcello remained silent; and Jack, although his hands and fingers drummed the steering wheel, also said nothing. In the silence, the drumming echoed through the car and out the windows to the harbor.

"We argued because she had decided to stop seeing me. I thought Anthony had stopped her, and I was driving away, angrier at him than I should have been. I hoped she would call out to bring me back. She didn't. Then I saw what happened behind me in the mirror. Jack, you did, too."

"Christ, you were about to drive away! I've never forgotten that."

Sonny nodded. "A horse, a wagon, and two bodies — hers, yours — flying to the curb on opposite sides. I heard it all, too. The wagon, the hooves, your mother's screams. They have tortured me more than what I saw."

Sonny shook his head, resolutely, and continued. "I could have beeped the horn, I could have opened the door and shouted. I could have run toward you to push you both out of the way. I did nothing. I froze and let myself watch."

"Jesus," Jack said.

"She had resolved to stay with Anthony to work things out. I felt abandoned. That was all. And for that I failed her — and sinned against God."

Marcello turned to Jack, who struggled to look at the road. For a long time they stared out the car windows as the sky grew darker and lights began to glow in the harbor across the way.

"What did your grandfather say to you about all this up on the mountain?" Sonny asked.

"I don't want to talk about that now."

Jack pointed to the tape recorder, motionless on the seat beside him. "Your words are safe, Marcello. They won't leave this car without that thing on."

"It's too embarrassing, Dad."

"If Anthony said she did that on purpose," Sonny said, "it was to excuse himself. She wanted freedom — perhaps from me that day, but also from her husband — and maybe others. But she wanted to give Anthony one last try. In those days there was little else a woman could do. Your grandmother appreciated men who understood that."

"Did you?"

Sonny looked at Marcello, staring for a full minute at him and then at Jack. Sadly, he shook his head.

"Not in my family, not with Lina," he said. "I failed there, too. But you wouldn't today — would you?"

Marcello said nothing. Jack still concentrated on the road. Sonny counted the sharp curves, while looking at the heads of the two men in the front seat. Neither moved.

"Margo," Jack whispered, swallowing.

"You made her unhappy," Sonny said, "as I did my own wife. My mother showed me that."

Marcello shifted in his seat and rubbed his palms together. Without a word, he clicked open the recorder, pulled out the cassette, took the notebooks and letters from the seat beside him, and, in a sudden, genuine fury, hurled them through the open window. Grappling for them as they left the car, Sonny gasped, his head pounding as he watched the papers sail with the wind, slide across the rocks, and then, blossoming like parachutes, float and spiral slowly toward the sea.

"There's nothing there, Sonny, nothing useful anyhow. Just a bunch of rants about other people's failures. If you want to speak more about these things, I'll be there, without a machine, to hear it."

"I will, too," Jack said. "I'm not sure my father ever got things right — about you, my mother, or anyone else."

Sonny shook his head. "Again — after more than a thousand times."

Marcello grinned. Sonny fidgeted as he saw them round another curve and head into a straightaway. Jack's fingers came back, walked along the seatback, took Sonny's, and, as the car descended toward the bay, held them all together, carefully.

Sighing, Sonny drew on his cigar.

ASHES

31.

"We were all slighted in those days, some of us more than others," Sonny said. "We just kept on working and didn't think about it."

He and Marcello settled into their room, high above the main streets of Potenza, just a few hours south of Naples. "Even Carmine and Anthony felt it. So we sinned to get even and felt bad about it later. We didn't know any better."

A television announcer's voice blared hoarsely through the wall from the room next door, and footsteps pounded up and down the hall outside. Cyclists, participating in a race from Naples to Bari, spoke and guffawed loudly above the footsteps. Sonny opened his leather valise and pulled out the urn of Modestina's ashes.

"Uncle Sonny. . . ."

"'Uncle?' — You're back to that again."

Marcello hesitated.

"Call me what you want. It doesn't matter. You can believe your grandfather, if you want. That's fine. I know where you come from. Here." Sonny pounded on his chest.

"I suppose you do."

Marcello stood at the window, pointing toward the right, where Potenza's cemetery lay in the distance. Brightly lit, bluish bulbs suspended against tombstones sent an eerie glow into the early dawn. The cemetery rested on a little dirt road, a footpath really, lined with shacks and huts, near where Sonny's mother, Modestina, had been born. Just beyond it, in the distance, the fires of a chemical factory burned into the sky. A blue flame of gas sputtered from a pipe well above the town.

Sonny insisted on driving up there after dinner the night before to visit a gathering of Salvaggis and Maresciallos settled into the earth. Homey, distant names he had heard from his mother lay frozen and shadowed in marble, with an occasional plastic flower floating above an inserted sepia photo much like his father's. But they found no Giovanni, no Battaglia.

The graves looked stark despite the decorations. A cool breeze blowing from the mountains beyond them scattered birds, papers, and plastic flowers along an even starker plain. Squawking birds, "nighthawks," Jack said, crossed and re-crossed the blue-black sky and seemed to shriek out warnings of betrayal. Suddenly a woman, short, hunch-backed, leaning on a wooden cane entered the cemetery. *Strega,* Sonny thought, despite the sympathy her struggling, shuffling gait brought to him. He glanced at Marcello, who immediately left his side and walked toward the woman, offering his hand on her arm for support.

"My son," Jack said, smiling, and he left Sonny's side to help the woman too.

"*Americani,*" she whispered with a shy smile toward Sonny. "*Che bellezzi giovani,*" she added. "Such beautiful young boys."

She paused before a gathering of tombstones, two or three with the Salvaggi name. Sonny studied her face, hoping for some slight sign of family resemblance. But her pale, wrinkled skin, solemn blue eyes, and yellow-gray hair offered no obvious clue. Her voice, throaty but with a high nasal rasp, hinted at his mother, Modestina, yet Sonny doubted his aural memory after so many years.

"*Mia famiglia,*" she muttered, waving her cane vaguely before her. Sonny looked at the tombstones and felt something shrivel up inside.

"Salvaggi?"

She shook her head.

"*Tutti.*"

Sonny glanced at her milky blue eyes and wondered whether she could read the names. "*Sono Franco,*" he said, "*figlio da Modestina Salvaggi. Habita qui vicino.*"

"*Non lo conosco,*" she said. "She isn't here."

Sonny moved closer, laying his hand on her arm which trembled on the cane.

With a shrug and a sickening sense of doom, he saw her eyes look up, past, then through him as she shook her head and turned toward another group of stones. "*Mia famiglia,*" she responded. Her clothes smelled of garlic and warm hallways, the black and gray print of her dress a somber contrast to the light sparkling on her hair. Sonny pulled out the photograph of Giovanni, flattened it against his chest, and held it very close to her face. She looked past it, then seemed to inhale suddenly, and turned away.

"*Conosce?*"

He handed it to Marcello, who smoothed it again and held it erect against his chest. Jack smiled and looked up the hill toward the town. He held up his hands before his eyes.

"*Non poso.*" She put her hands before her own eyes and asked for the name of the man in the photo. Sonny pronounced it slowly and watched her chin sink slowly toward her breast as she pulled her arm from him and started to walk past them toward another part of the grounds. She shook her head.

"*È securo?*" He asked, his Italian escaping him as if it were his own language. "You never knew a man named Giovanni Battaglia? *È mio babbo.*"

She stopped, looked through him, then shook her head again. "*È morto.* He came here many, many years ago, made many, many friends — many girlfriends — and disappeared. No one ever saw him again. No one wanted to."

Her face contorted into a painful, sullen mask; her hand fluttered in the air as if waving away some mist. Sonny wanted to ask more, but he sensed an awful anguish that questions about his mother and this man would revive in this woman's soul. Looking at Jack and Marcello, he shook his head, but even after his polite thank you, she continued down the path, mumbling and staring at the distant sky.

32.

They decided to go back to the hotel where, this morning, from the window, Marcello pointed to a quiet, almost bucolic scene with none of the nightmarish shrieks and gloom of the night before. Still the sad image of the little humpbacked woman filled their heads.

"I want to find out more, about all this," Marcello said. "Not only about the town and those mountains, but how we got from here to there — home, I mean — what things led up to it."

"Your grandmother Lillian was from up north, you know — not down here. Tuscany — and even Ireland."

"I know, I know, cool intelligence, just like my mother. My grandfather was actually proud of that — that my father had actually picked her."

"Your mother has spirit, too," Sonny said, smiling. "Also like your grandmother."

He reached down, slid his chair along the floor, and lifted his mother's urn to his lap. Glazed white, without an identifying mark on its outer surface, the soft, pot-bellied shape possessed a certain maternal quality, not at all like Sonny's mother. The presence of human ashes inside, especially Modestina's, especially an unknown portion of her, here in Potenza, struck Sonny as very unreal. He pursed his lips, sucked his teeth, but made no other sound. Marcello took the urn from his lap and carefully placed it on a table.

"You have an inheritance coming from me, you know," Sonny said to him. "When you're thirty. I mean the Garibaldi Club, near where your grandmother and Jack. . . . It has the zoning and land necessary for a big expansion now. It could be a new, modern facility and still keep its traditional name. I built the second Garibaldi Club, after Carmine. You can build the third. Or destroy it and do something else." He laughed. "Maybe more of my wind-driven condos in memory of your grandfather."

Marcello waved. "I'll leave that stuff for others," he said, smiling.

"Hey, anything is possible, my boy, even leaving it as is. Your father certainly doesn't want it. Franco and Sunnyview have no use for it. Pretty soon I won't even remember what it is. It's a family structure, my gift to you — and your children. Tell your future wife that. Tell your mother. It is my gift to her through you. And the other, the little one. Tina."

Marcello nodded and smiled. After a brief knock, the door to the room opened, and Jack ambled in, sitting with a sigh on a chair near the bed. He had jogged down the hill into town just after breakfast, searching for signs of the Maresciallo or Salvaggi presence above doors and on storefronts. "I want to see some names, somewhere among the living," he had said as he had left in his running shoes and shorts. There was a pharmacy carrying the name Salvaggi painted on the windows, and the owner, Jack had found out, now lived in a villa near Siena.

Sonny paid no attention; it was old news to him. What's more the Battaglia name never came up. "Do you understand me, Marcello?" he asked. "I want to leave you and your family something. It comes from your great grandfather, Carmine, through me, not your grandfather, and I don't want it to be lost."

Marcello nodded. "Thanks, Sonny, but I'm not the landowning type. Or a builder. Perhaps my mother. . . ."

"I've wanted to thank Carmine — and your great grandmother, Carmella — for years; show my appreciation for taking care of me. And my mother."

Jack said nothing. Humming softly against the sound of the announcer from next door, he shifted in his chair when Marcello tapped his shoulder.

"My father's here now, Uncle Sonny. We can both listen; we're ready to hear all about it — that day with my grandmother — and everything else."

Sonny rose, shaking his head. "No more," he said. Swiping his fingers beneath his chin, he walked slowly to the window, swung it outward, and, hands shaking, fumbled with the urn of ashes on the nearby table.

"Sonny. . . ."

The whispered syllables sounded shrill as Jack and Marcello stepped to the window quickly and held him by either arm. "Hey, I'm not throwing it, or dropping it. And I'm certainly not ready to jump." Sonny smiled. "Put it back in the valise for me, Marcello, to return it — to Pennsylvania, with the rocks and the soil behind the Garibaldi Club. My mother belongs there, just as you do. Just as Anthony and Carmine did. With Lillian — probably I do, too."

Looking in the mirror, he took off his hat and waved to the blue-lit cemetery in the distance.

Lillian . . . Anthony . . . Giovanni? . . .

Footsteps, he was thinking, wheels, and especially the years. Everything, everything gathers speed. . . .

EPILOGUE: A WORLD MADE NEW

33.

"Carmine Maresciallo and Son.
Quarry: Shale, Slate, Brick, Mortar.
Since 1901."

The truck and pickup still stand there. Anthony kept the shop's hand-painted sign hammered to the back wall of the family garage, facing the mountain that had been the source of all their holdings. Now, when Jack stood with Marcello and Tina and looked at that pile of rock, its jagged, hollowed out peak, he felt bitter, though he too knew it had provided support once for his grandparents, parents, many community people, and him. Thanks to Anthony, only a silhouette remained.

Late in the 1880s Jack's grandfather, Carmine, eldest son of a poor socialist farmer, packed a lunch of his possessions, cheese, a stick of bread, a small ring of sausage, and trudged out of the tiny Basilicatan village of Frigio Valfortore, in the region of Potenza, Italy. He marched over the mountains toward the sea, slept, dreamed, waited for a week in the hills around the Amalfi coast, and, hiding in the dark hold of an English freighter (with just a loaf of bread now, stolen from a Neapolitan baker the morning before he boarded), set sail for the United States. Sweating, filthy, starved, and no longer dreaming, he arrived fifteen days later, blinded by the light pouring through the open hatch, and found himself too weak to move, much less leave the hold of the ship.

Carmine thought he would never touch land again, but a friendly New Englander, Ensign Anthony Elmo, a broad hulk of a seaman, "My double saint," Carmine used to say to people at the old Garibaldi Club, heard his moans and took pity.

"*Amico?*" Elmo said, walking through the gloom and hearing Carmine moaning. "*Che Amici?*"

"*Amici, sì! Sicuro! Sono amico, sì!*"

Carmine managed to croak the words aloud, though at the time he could barely raise his hand.

Stowaways brought rich bounties in those days, but Ensign Elmo fed Carmine below deck that afternoon, carried him ashore under the cover of night, dragged him through the streets like a drunk unable to find his way home, and installed him in a sailors' hotel in the port of Brooklyn. "We've all been there at one time, my friend," he said. "All of us are immigrants in some way, and these are some fish I give you to help you grow the corn." He handed Carmine money from his wallet for food, fresh clothing, American liquor, and more.

Ten days later, when Ensign Elmo's ship lifted anchor to return to the Mediterranean, Carmine left the room alone — calmer, stronger, truly a new man. He knew a few words of English and, thanks to Elmo, carried passable immigration papers, too. Gathering a pair of shoes into his second shirt, he hung the bundle over his shoulder and walked across the bridge, hearing the music of its massive cables in the wind that blew across the bay. Through the streets of Chinatown and into the narrow, winding lanes above Canal, he discovered familiar-sounding names, Posilippo, Farrara, and Misuriello, on mailboxes and window signs, and, as he had anticipated with such great joy, the familiar sound and language of home.

The very first day he began work as an apprentice to a shoemaker named Caserta. He cut and sewed leather for six months, grew restless and bored, then transferred his apprenticeship to a stone mason named Belvecchio, a man he had met over sandwiches at a corner tavern, and in whose home he would also meet Anthony's mother, Elena, and his step-mother, Carmella, the stone mason's daughters. A broadsheet Carmine tore down from a wall in the city had hung above his desk in the quarry shop:

> "Labor, white — $1.50 a day;
> Colored — $1.25 a day;
> Italian — $1.15."

"*Medigahn*," Carmine always said when he showed it to his grandson, Jack. With a nasty glint in his eye, as the boy sat on his knee, he added, "If they work, I pay the best wages in these mountains."

His scorn for that biased attitude nearly matched his disdain for the young country's attempts to imitate Italy, descending, he constantly reminded his grandson from a crumbled empire that once had ruled the world. Carmine shrugged, nodding at that broadsheet before them. He had made money and a life he never could have equaled back home, he admitted, but despite the eagle, the mighty dollar, and all the country's growing military power, he had to tell Jack that this nation had little maturity, and even less endurance. "Why? Grandpa . . . *Nonno?*"

Carmine nodded, grateful for the "*Nonno*" part. "Because they do not know how to suffer," he said. "Where are New York's marbles?" He would look at his grandson and shake his head. "New York buildings have been made to fall — to crack — at a certain pitch of sound."

Carmine. . . . If he complained too loudly and long about his adopted country, little Jack knew that his *nonna* Elena felt nearly the same — even more excluded, perhaps, because she was a woman who had little dealings with the outside world. Carmine refused to let her work, although she could shop and socialize as much as she wished. Still she eagerly left Manhattan with him in the early years. As more people descended from the boats in New York Harbor, wandered through Chinatown into the upper reaches of the city, Carmine and Elena felt less human and more like members of an expanding, shapeless herd. They hoped for acceptance outside the city. Staying in New Jersey for a time, they rented a small house on the periphery of Newark while Carmine worked the quarries in the surrounding Watchung Hills and Orange Mountains. But after many years, they both grew dissatisfied there, too, and Elena asked to move farther west, to the hills and mountains of Pennsylvania.

They conceived Anthony in May. With Elena full and confident that September, Carmine packed their belongings — bread, cheese, sausage, shirt, and shoes now grown to a small wagonful of possessions — and they followed the sun toward the Delaware. Years afterward, Carmine still talked about the beauty of that first passage, the lush, pine-topped mountains of western Jersey, hawks, wild turkeys, and ospreys circling them; the deer that crossed the wagon trails and stopped, trustingly, as Carmine described them, to observe a curiosity, two humans trailing behind them a pile of wood and cloth; and the Delaware River twisting in and around the mountains like a blue snake slithering to the ocean from the continent's heart. With a bowler sitting on his head, horse and wagon standing behind him, and Elena at his right arm, Carmine rode a ferry to the Pennsylvania side of the water. Setting up a tent in a settlement named Smithfield, he immediately began to search for land.

They had cash, well hidden, and in addition had arranged credit with a family bank in New York. They could buy property when they found it or order food and clothing should they run out. Elena, trusting, enjoyed the luck of agreeable dry weather as well as the surrounding natural beauty. Raised on the streets of lower Manhattan, she had never traveled above 14th Street, never visited Central Park, and had hardly experienced rock and grass without cement, brick, or slate outlining them.

In their riverside camp she started to sketch. Taking a piece of charred wood from the fire one morning, she began to draw the scene around them. Almost unconsciously, and to her happy surprise, mountains arose on the brown paper before her, oaks, fir trees, and bush took on harsh, thorny beauty, and animals bore the twitch of breath in their muzzles.

She had drawn very little before, no one in the Belvecchio family or her mother's had ever taken up a palette. Half-jokingly, she concluded that some ancient rush of Roman, or even Tuscan, blood in her arteries now guided her hand, though her family, like Carmine's, came from the south. She knew she could sing with just an average soprano voice, dance with elemental, but untutored grace, and, in addition to Italian, speak English, with a decent, but uneducated accent. Yet here in Penn's woods, with Jersey's hills across the water and very little New York education to fall back on, a certain magic appeared beneath her fingers. In a sense, Carmine always told people, flowing water and mountainous landscape, even more than carrying Anthony, brought his young wife to maturity.

Meanwhile, he sought to start his own business, a quarry, assuming the rocky resources of these mountains and what Carmine hoped would be a growing population of immigrants building homes, churches, and stores, would yield much needed family profit.

Kicking on the journey across New Jersey, Anthony now took up much of the space in their sleeping cot at night. At the end of the sixth month Elena grew weak. Although the weather remained mild for much of October, they decided to take caution and move out of their tent. Finding a small piece of land on the side of a tall hill (near the east side of Smithfield), Carmine split logs and built a cabin. He insulated it with clay and mud from the riverbanks. Through the intense snows and frost of that winter, Anthony grew large, ripened, and before the cabin fire on a windy, snowy February morning, dropped to earth like a fat seed in autumn.

With a calm that still surprised him years later, Carmine boiled water, pressed on Elena's abdomen, picked up his new son and cleaned him, then cut and tied the only share Anthony ever had on his mother's physical life.

"Bellezza moribonda," Carmine muttered, bitterly. "Dying beauty. The ghost rose on her cheeks from his very first cry."

She remained, barely conscious until a few hours later. Anthony howled through most of that spring and summer, driving his father out of the cabin and back to Manhattan where Carmine showed the Belvecchios their new grandson and convinced his sister-in-law Carmella to return to the mountains with him. Wedding photographs show her to look very much like Elena, slightly smaller and much more fair. In the country home Carmine led her to, Carmella missed her family and, like her sister before her, began to sketch to fill in the time.

Carmine logged for nearly a year, and finally, as Anthony crawled and toddled around the cabin, found a piece of rocky land that he could afford. He borrowed tools from the Belvecchio masonry in New York City, bought old machinery from a former employer in New Jersey, and started mining. Cutters needed limestone for grave markers and railroad bridges throughout the Poconos, and, as he had guessed, Carmine soon discovered a steady stream of immigrants behind him. They poured from New York harbor, crossed westward toward the Jersey hills, and rode into Pennsylvania to board a boat on the Delaware, down river toward Philadelphia, or — some of them — northward for the Pocono Mountains. Carmine hired a few, one, a bright, young man — Giovanni, though he always called him Sonny — who became a manager of the mine; Sonny's *amica*, Modestina, who cleaned the house for years and then brought food for him and his workers until she bore her boy. They — and others like them — remained, started farms, raised homes, erected churches throughout the Depression and even into World War II. As it prospered, Maresciallo's Quarry made Carmine a major employer in Smithfield, and his wealth increased as streets and buildings multiplied. His ground lime worked as fertilizer, his slate lined neighborhood roofs; as if by writ, his blocks of stone and brick transformed bell towers and buildings into sacred images. Even the Garibaldi Club was built through Carmine's charity, and with all that, Anthony, his only son, also grew.

Then:

"Dad, I'd like you to meet my very good friend, Lillian, an artist. And teacher."

Carmine leaned back, squinted, noting auburn hair, a friendly, welcoming smile, and the fierce intelligence in a pair of Irish emerald eyes. "*Dio mio,*" he said aloud, seeing his bright, white hair and mustache shine in her pupils. "How did this happen?"

"Watch it, *Babbo*, her name is O'Clare," Anthony said, grinning.

"But, I assure you, only half of her is Irish. The rest is pure Umbrian gold."

"Quick, take her to your mother and introduce them. Go to the Salvaggis, Sonny *Figlio* and Modestina, too. Introduce them. We must show her how well southern Italians can live in this country."

Lillian smiled as Carmine reached out to take her hand and, bowing gently, kissed it. Laughing, Anthony put his arm about her shoulders, pressed his lips to her cheek, and started toward the house.

"*Uomo.*" Carmine whispered, as he watched them cross the graveled road then walk across the lawn toward his own massive walnut door. "*Mio figlio.*"

He looked to the sky and turned from it, aware of the sudden image of something precious passing.

"And I have just now begun to live," Carmine muttered.

He lifted a shovel and a pick. Hoisting them to his shoulder, he trudged down the footpath toward a pile of rocks.

Published by Bordighera, Inc., an independently owned not-for-profit scholarly organization that has no legal affiliation with the University of Central Florida and The John D. Calandra Italian American Institute, Queens College/CUNY.

BEA TUSIANI, *con amore*, Vol. 35, Memoir, $19

FLAVIA BRIZIO-SKOV, Ed., *Reconstructing Societies in the Aftermath of War*, Vol. 34, History, $30

TAMBURRI, et al., Eds., *Italian Cultural Studies 2001*, Vol. 33, Essays, $18

ELIZABETH G. MESSINA, Ed., *In Our Own Voices*, Vol. 32, Italian American Studies, $25

STANISLAO G. PUGLIESE, *Desperate Inscriptions*, Vol. 31, History, $12

HOSTERT & TAMBURRI, Eds., *Screening Ethnicity*, Vol. 30, Italian American Culture, $25

G. PARATI & B. LAWTON, Eds., *Italian Cultural Studies*, Vol. 29, Essays, $18

HELEN BAROLINI, *More Italian Hours*, Vol. 28, Fiction, $16

FRANCO NASI, Ed., *Intorno alla Via Emilia*, Vol. 27, Culture, $16

ARTHUR L. CLEMENTS, *The Book of Madness & Love*, Vol. 26, Poetry, $10

JOHN CASEY, et al., *Imagining Humanity*, Vol. 25, Interdisciplinary Studies, $18

ROBERT LIMA, *Sardinia/Sardegna*, Vol. 24, Poetry, $10

DANIELA GIOSEFFI, *Going On*, Vol. 23, Poetry, $10

ROSS TALARICO, *The Journey Home*, Vol. 22, Poetry, $12

EMANUEL DI PASQUALE, *The Silver Lake Love Poems*, Vol. 21, Poetry, $7

JOSEPH TUSIANI, *Ethnicity*, Vol. 20, Poetry, $12

JENNIFER LAGIER, *Second Class Citizen*, Vol. 19, Poetry, $8

FELIX STEFANILE, *The Country of Absence*, Vol. 18, Poetry, $9

PHILIP CANNISTRARO, *Blackshirts*, Vol. 17, History, $12

LUIGI RUSTICHELLI, Ed., *Seminario sul racconto*, Vol. 16, Narrative, $10

LEWIS TURCO, *Shaking the Family Tree*, Vol. 15, Memoirs, $9

LUIGI RUSTICHELLI, Ed., *Seminario sulla drammaturgia*, Vol. 14, Theater/Essays, $10

FRED GARDAPHÈ, *Moustache Pete is Dead! Long Live Moustache Pete!*, Vol. 13, Oral Literature, $10

JONE GAILLARD CORSI, *Il libretto d'autore, 1860–1930*, Vol. 12, Criticism, $17

HELEN BAROLINI, *Chiaroscuro: Essays of Identity*, Vol. 11, Essays, $15

PICARAZZI & FEINSTEIN, Eds., *An African Harlequin in Milan*, Vol. 10, Theater/Essays, $15

JOSEPH RICAPITO, *Florentine Streets & Other Poems*, Vol. 9, Poetry, $9

FRED MISURELLA, *Short Time*, Vol. 8, Novella, $7

NED CONDINI, *Quartettsatz*, Vol. 7, Poetry, $7

ANTHONY TAMBURRI, Ed., *Fuori: Essays by Italian/American Lesbians and Gays*, Vol. 6, Essays, $10

ANTONIO GRAMSCI, P. Verdicchio, Trans. & Intro. , *The Southern Question*, Vol. 5, Social Criticism, $5

DANIELA GIOSEFFI, *Word Wounds & Water Flowers*, Vol. 4, Poetry, $8

WILEY FEINSTEIN, *Humility's Deceit: Calvino Reading Ariosto Reading Calvino*, Vol. 3, Criticism, $10

PAOLO A. GIORDANO, Ed., *Joseph Tusiani: Poet, Translator, Humanist*, Vol. 2, Criticism, $25

ROBERT VISCUSI, *Oration Upon the Most Recent Death of Christopher Columbus*, Vol. 1, Poetry, $3

www.ingramcontent.com/pod-product-compliance
Lightning Source LLC
Chambersburg PA
CBHW021008180626
46814CB00003B/1188